L B
LITTLE, BROWN
AND COMPANY
NEW YORK
BOSTON

SPIRIT

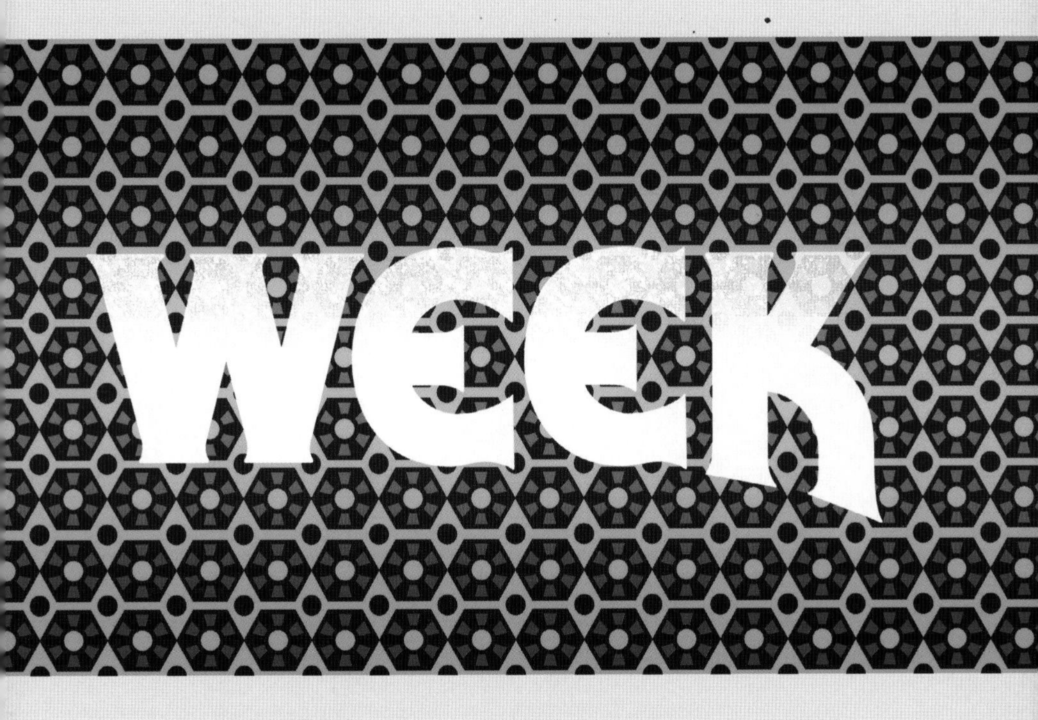

by IRA MARCKS

Colors by Addison Duke

About This Book

This book was edited by Andrea Colvin and designed by Megan McLaughlin. The production was supervised by Bernadette Flinn, and the production editor was Jake Regier. The text was set in Amity Island, and the display type is Linotype Typo American.

This book is a work of fiction. Names, characters, places, and incidents are the product of the author's imagination or are used fictitiously. Any resemblance to actual events, locales, or persons, living or dead, is coincidental.

Little, Brown and Company
Hachette Book Group
1290 Avenue of the Americas, New York, NY 10104
Visit us at LBYR.com

First Edition: October 2022

Little, Brown and Company is a division of Hachette Book Group, Inc.
The Little, Brown name and logo are trademarks of Hachette Book Group, Inc.

The publisher is not responsible for websites (or their content) that are not owned by the publisher.

Library of Congress Cataloging-in-Publication Data
Names: Marcks, Ira, author, illustrator.
Title: Spirit week / by Ira Marcks.
Description: First edition. | New York: Little, Brown and Company, 2022. | Audience: Ages 12 & up. | Summary: Two people, aspiring filmmaker Elijah and thirteen-year-old tutor Suzy, are invited to a largely deserted hotel in Estes Park, Colorado, to make a film about reclusive horror author Jack Axworth and tutor his son, Danny; but the situation is not as expected: Jack is suffering from early onset dementia and, convinced that his books have released evil, is trying to buy up and destroy them as well as the hotel he lives in—but nobody is quite what they seem, and soon the whole project starts to resemble one of Jack's horror novels.
Identifiers: LCCN 2021041039 | ISBN 9780316277945 (hardcover) | ISBN 9780316278065 (trade paperback) | ISBN 9780316278218 (ebook)
Subjects: LCSH: Graphic novels. | Horror tales. | Novelists—Comic books, strips, etc. | Novelists—Juvenile fiction. | Motion picture producers and directors—Comic books, strips, etc. | Motion picture producers and directors—Juvenile fiction. | Secrecy—Comic books, strips, etc. | Secrecy—Juvenile fiction. | Estes Park (Colo.)—Comic books, strips, etc. | Estes Park (Colo.)—Juvenile fiction. | CYAC: Graphic novels. | Horror stories. | Secrets—Fiction. | Estes Park (Colo.)—Fiction. | LCGFT: Graphic novels. | Horror fiction.
Classification: LCC PZ7.7.M3378 Sp 2022 | DDC 741.5/973—dc23
LC record available at https://lccn.loc.gov/2021041039

ISBNs: 978-0-316-27794-5 (hardcover), 978-0-316-27806-5 (pbk.), 978-0-316-27821-8 (ebook), 978-0-316-33290-3 (ebook), 978-0-316-33299-6 (ebook)

Printed in Germany

Mohn Media

Hardcover: 10 9 8 7 6 5 4 3 2 1
Paperback: 10 9 8 7 6 5 4 3 2 1

To Dad

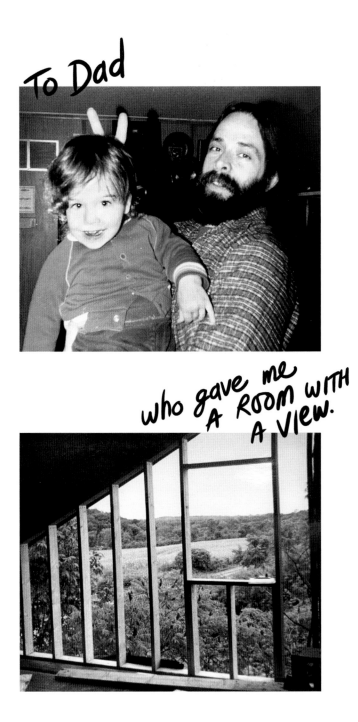

who gave me A ROOM WITH A VIEW.

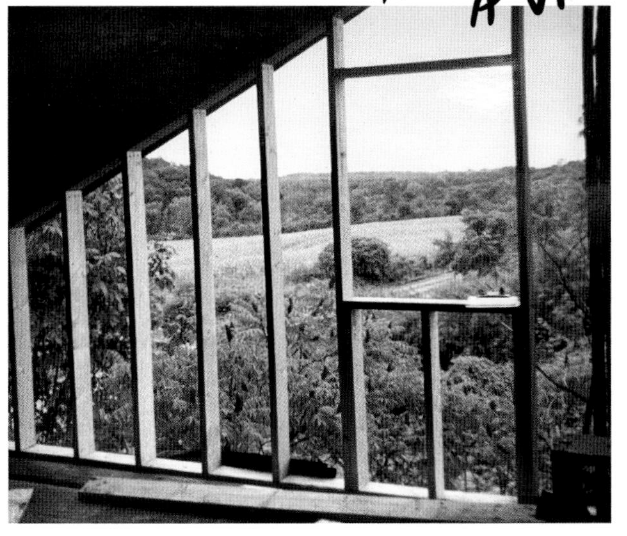

PATENT 10135

PATENT 10135

STATE OF COLORADO
7,800 FEET
ABOVE SEA LEVEL
NAVD 88
GEOLOGICAL MARKER

DRIP

CHICAGO WORLDS FAIR
BRAZIL
BALI

GIRL IN THE CAVE
BY SUZY H.

TINK TINK

SRACK

LONDON
POMPEI
CHICAGO
BRAZIL

THE
UNDERLOOK HOTEL
ESTES PARK, COLORADO

```
 ::::::::    :::    :::   ::::    :::   :::::::::         :::       :::   :::
:+:    :+:   :+:    :+:   :+:+:   :+:   :+:    :+:      :+: :+:     :+:   :+:
+:+          +:+    +:+   :+:+:+  +:+   +:+    +:+     +:+   +:+     +:+ +:+
+#++:++#++   +#+    +:+   +#+ +:+ +#+   +#+    +:+    +#++:++#++:     +#++:
       +#+   +#+    +#+   +#+  +#+#+#   +#+    +#+    +#+     +#+      +#+
#+#    #+#   #+#    #+#   #+#   #+#+#   #+#    #+#    #+#     #+#      #+#
 ########     ########    ###    ####   #########     ###     ###      ###

              ::::::::    :::    :::   ::::    :::   :::::::::         :::       :::   :::
             :+:    :+:   :+:    :+:   :+:+:   :+:   :+:    :+:      :+: :+:     :+:   :+:
             +:+          +:+    +:+   :+:+:+  +:+   +:+    +:+     +:+   +:+     +:+ +:+
             +#++:++#++   +#+    +:+   +#+ +:+ +#+   +#+    +:+    +#++:++#++:     +#++:
                    +#+   +#+    +#+   +#+  +#+#+#   +#+    +#+    +#+     +#+      +#+
             #+#    #+#   #+#    #+#   #+#   #+#+#   #+#    #+#    #+#     #+#      #+#
              ########     ########    ###    ####   #########     ###     ###      ###

                           ::::::::    :::    :::   ::::    :::   :::::::::         :::       :::   :::
                          :+:    :+:   :+:    :+:   :+:+:   :+:   :+:    :+:      :+: :+:     :+:   :+:
                          +:+          +:+    +:+   :+:+:+  +:+   +:+    +:+     +:+   +:+     +:+ +:+
                          +#++:++#++   +#+    +:+   +#+ +:+ +#+   +#+    +:+    +#++:++#++:     +#++:
                                 +#+   +#+    +#+   +#+  +#+#+#   +#+    +#+    +#+     +#+      +#+
                          #+#    #+#   #+#    #+#   #+#   #+#+#   #+#    #+#    #+#     #+#      #+#
                           ########     ########    ###    ####   #########     ###     ###      ###

                                        ::::::::    :::    :::   ::::    :::   :::::::::         :::       :::   :::
                                       :+:    :+:   :+:    :+:   :+:+:   :+:   :+:    :+:      :+: :+:     :+:   :+:
                                       +:+          +:+    +:+   :+:+:+  +:+   +:+    +:+     +:+   +:+     +:+ +:+
                                       +#++:++#++   +#+    +:+   +#+ +:+ +#+   +#+    +:+    +#++:++#++:     +#++:
                                              +#+   +#+    +#+   +#+  +#+#+#   +#+    +#+    +#+     +#+      +#+
                                       #+#    #+#   #+#    #+#   #+#   #+#+#   #+#    #+#    #+#     #+#      #+#
                                        ########     ########    ###    ####   #########     ###     ###      ###

 ::::::::    :::    :::   ::::    :::   :::::::::         :::       :::   :::
:+:    :+:   :+:    :+:   :+:+:   :+:   :+:    :+:      :+: :+:     :+:   :+:
+:+          +:+    +:+   :+:+:+  +:+   +:+    +:+     +:+   +:+     +:+ +:+
+#++:++#++   +#+    +:+   +#+ +:+ +#+   +#+    +:+    +#++:++#++:     +#++:
       +#+   +#+    +#+   +#+  +#+#+#   +#+    +#+    +#+     +#+      +#+
#+#    #+#   #+#    #+#   #+#   #+#+#   #+#    #+#    #+#     #+#      #+#
 ########     ########    ###    ####   #########     ###     ###      ###

              ::::::::    :::    :::   ::::    :::   :::::::::         :::       :::   :::
             :+:    :+:   :+:    :+:   :+:+:   :+:   :+:    :+:      :+: :+:     :+:   :+:
             +:+          +:+    +:+   :+:+:+  +:+   +:+    +:+     +:+   +:+     +:+ +:+
             +#++:++#++   +#+    +:+   +#+ +:+ +#+   +#+    +:+    +#++:++#++:     +#++:
                    +#+   +#+    +#+   +#+  +#+#+#   +#+    +#+    +#+     +#+      +#+
             #+#    #+#   #+#    #+#   #+#   #+#+#   #+#    #+#    #+#     #+#      #+#
              ########     ########    ###    ####   #########     ###     ###      ###

                           ::::::::    :::    :::   ::::    :::   :::::::::         :::       :::   :::
                          :+:    :+:   :+:    :+:   :+:+:   :+:   :+:    :+:      :+: :+:     :+:   :+:
                          +:+          +:+    +:+   :+:+:+  +:+   +:+    +:+     +:+   +:+     +:+ +:+
                          +#++:++#++   +#+    +:+   +#+ +:+ +#+   +#+    +:+    +#++:++#++:     +#++:
                                 +#+   +#+    +#+   +#+  +#+#+#   +#+    +#+    +#+     +#+      +#+
                          #+#    #+#   #+#    #+#   #+#   #+#+#   #+#    #+#    #+#     #+#      #+#
                           ########     ########    ###    ####   #########     ###     ###      ###

                                        ::::::::    :::    :::   ::::    :::   :::::::::         :::       :::   :::
                                       :+:    :+:   :+:    :+:   :+:+:   :+:   :+:    :+:      :+: :+:     :+:   :+:
                                       +:+          +:+    +:+   :+:+:+  +:+   +:+    +:+     +:+   +:+     +:+ +:+
                                       +#++:++#++   +#+    +:+   +#+ +:+ +#+   +#+    +:+    +#++:++#++:     +#++:
                                              +#+   +#+    +#+   +#+  +#+#+#   +#+    +#+    +#+     +#+      +#+
                                       #+#    #+#   #+#    #+#   #+#   #+#+#   #+#    #+#    #+#     #+#      #+#
                                        ########     ########    ###    ####   #########     ###     ###      ###

 ::::::::    :::    :::   ::::    :::   :::::::::         :::       :::   :::
:+:    :+:   :+:    :+:   :+:+:   :+:   :+:    :+:      :+: :+:     :+:   :+:
+:+          +:+    +:+   :+:+:+  +:+   +:+    +:+     +:+   +:+     +:+ +:+
+#++:++#++   +#+    +:+   +#+ +:+ +#+   +#+    +:+    +#++:++#++:     +#++:
       +#+   +#+    +#+   +#+  +#+#+#   +#+    +#+    +#+     +#+      +#+
#+#    #+#   #+#    #+#   #+#   #+#+#   #+#    #+#    #+#     #+#      #+#
 ########     ########    ###    ####   #########     ###     ###      ###
```

THUMP

THUMPTHUM

TAXI
007-981
THUMPTHUMPTHUMPTHUMP

ARE WE ALMOST THERE?
CLOSE. STILL PASSIN' THROUGH BIG THOMPSON CANYON.
THUMPTHUMPTHUMPTHUMP

WE'LL BE IN ESTES PARK SOON IF THE WEATHER HOLDS. FIRST TIME IN COLORADO, YEAH?
YUP! I'M FROM BOSTON. WE DON'T HAVE CANYONS OR ANYTHING THAT LOOKS LIKE THIS!

SPEAKING OF, I SHOULD BE GETTING SOME B-ROLL.
FILM
ZODAK
FILM

BOSTON, HUH? WHAT ARE YA DOING OUT HERE?
I'M FILMING A DOCUMENTARY!

ABOUT THE PARK?
NO, ABOUT A WRITER.
ZODAK
VIIBRA-COLOR

A WRITER? THEY FAMOUS?
THEY USED TO BE.

WHAT HAPPENED?
THAT'S WHAT I'M GOING TO FIND OUT.

MINIATURE
GOLF
CLOSED 4
S3ASON
STOMP EM
YETIS!
MINE
BARLOWE
SKI
HIDDEN VALLEY
9 MILES WEST of ESTES PARK
MOTEL
VACANCY
COTTAGES
ON THE RIVER
KICHENETTE!
ROCK CANYON
RANCH
ESTES PARK
CITY LIMIT
ELEV 7522 FT

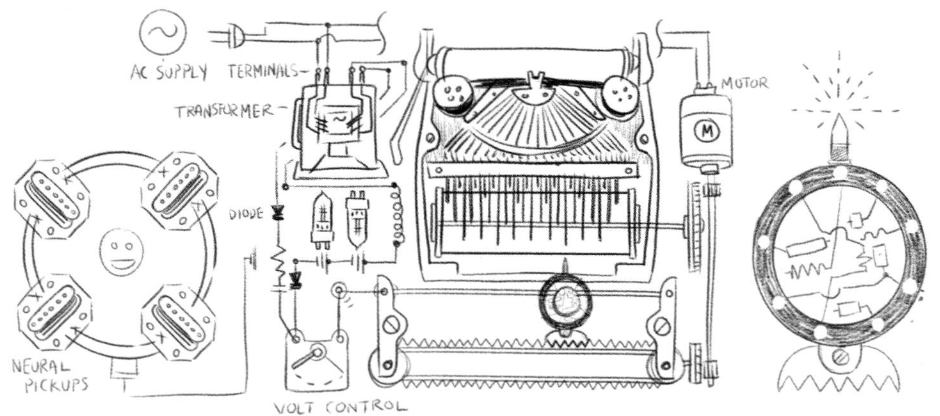
AC SUPPLY
TERMINALS
TRANSFORMER
MOTOR
DIODE
NEURAL PICKUPS
VOLT CONTROL

RELAYS
DIODES
AK LER
SALE
YOU READY, SUZY?
AS I'LL EVER BE, MOM.

OOPS.
BZZT
SALE
DIODES
AKLER

THUMP! THUMP!
ALL RIGHT, ALL RIGHT!
DON'T BLOW A FUSE!
I TELL YA, SUZ, SOMEDAY WE'RE GONNA LIVE IN A BUILDING WIRED FOR THIS CENTURY.

HM.

LOWER THE VOLTAGE. IT'LL WORK.

WHERE'D YOU GET THE TYPEWRITER, ANYWAY?
PAWNSHOP.
IT BELONGED TO JACK AXWORTH! GUESS HE'S OFFICIALLY RETIRED NOW.

HIS TYPEWRITER WAS JUST SITTING IN A PAWNSHOP?
I GOT IT FOR A STEAL. GUY DIDN'T KNOW WHAT HE HAD–
BUT I'D RECOGNIZE JACK'S OLD AKLER ANYWHERE.
RELAYS
BATTERIES
DIODES
AKLER

THOUGHT I'D GIVE IT A SECOND LIFE. TURN IT INTO SOMETHING FUN FOR THE TOURISTS, YOU KNOW?
AKLER
STOMP'EM!

YOU MEAN THE UNDERLURKERS.
WHATEVER WE CALL 'EM—
THEY PAY THE BILLS.

I'M GOING TO BE UP AT THE HOTEL ALL WEEK.
MAYBE I CAN DIG UP SOME OTHER JACK AXWORTH ARTIFACTS FOR THE SHOP.

YOU'RE GOING THERE TO TUTOR HIS SON, NOT TO SNOOP AROUND.
RELAX, MOM, I'M KIDDING.

IT BUGS YOU THAT I TOOK THE JOB, DOESN'T IT?
YOU KNOW I DON'T LIKE THAT OLD HOTEL.

AND YOU KNOW I NEED THE MONEY FOR THE COMPETITION.
I HAVE TO DEFEND MY TITLE!
SEE, THIS IS WHY I DIDN'T SAY ANYTHING.

YOU'RE ALWAYS CHASING TROPHIES!
IT'S WINTER-BREAK WEEK. WHY DON'T YOU TRY BEING A KID FOR A WHILE—
OUCH!

DARN DIODE!
OK, FINE. I WAS GOING TO DO SOME READING TONIGHT—
BUT WE CAN, I DUNNO, WATCH A MOVIE.

REALLY? CAN WE MAKE POPCORN?
FLIP!
WHATEVER YOU WANT, MOM.

OH, LET'S WATCH *GONE WITH THE WIND.* IT USED TO BE YOUR FAVORITE!
TOO LONG. I HAVE TO GET UP EARLY.

FLIP!
SUSANNA HESS—YOU DON'T KNOW HOW TO HAVE FUN.

I AM HAVING FUN.

HONK

RADIO GHOST
HONK

HA HA.
THIS IS AWESOME!
YER ALL LUCKY IT ISN'T HUNTING SEASON.

HEY, IT'S BEEN A FUN RIDE! I GOT SOME REALLY COOL FOOTAGE.

LOOKS LIKE I CAN WALK FROM HERE.

WALK? WHERE ARE YA STAYING, ANYWAY?

THE UNDERLOOK HOTEL!

THE UNDERLOOK?
YER PULLING MY LEG.
NOPE!
PRETTY COOL, HUH?
FARE

SEE YOU LATER.
YEAH, SEE YA, KID.

HEY, BE CAREFUL OUT THERE!

I'M FROM BOSTON, REMEMBER? I'M NOT AFRAID OF A LITTLE SNOW!
I'M NOT TALKIN' 'BOUT THE SNOW.

THERE HE IS!
ELIJAH JONES!
HUH?

DONNA DUNKIN WITH KRKY 13: ROCKY MOUNTAIN NEWS.
13 KRKY

I'D LIKE TO ASK YOU A FEW QUESTIONS.
13 KRKY

BCA TK-80.
THE LATEST PORTABLE BROADCAST-QUALITY TELEVISION CAMERA—
MR. JONES!
UH, YEAH?

WHAT'S IT LIKE TO BE THE UNDERLOOK HOTEL'S FIRST GUEST IN FOUR YEARS?
I DUNNO, I JUST GOT HERE.

HOW DO YOU KNOW—
JACK AXWORTH?

IF IT'S THAT REPORTER AGAIN, TELL 'EM TO BUZZ OFF.
IT'S HER, ALL RIGHT. BUT NOW SHE'S CHASING AFTER SOME BOY.

UH-OH, HE SAW ME.

RADIO GHOST
HI, HELLO?
ARE YOU OPEN?!

I'M SORRY, WE'RE CLOSED ON SUNDAYS.

GEESH, SUZY. GIVE HIM A BREAK— HE'S A KID.
WHAT? I'M JUST FOLLOWING THE RULES!

DING!
THANK YOU!

JUST A FEW QUESTIONS.
13 KRKY

COME BACK
13 KRKY

THANKS! I REALLY DON'T LIKE BEING ON CAMERA.
SHE CALLED YOU MR. JONES.

ARE YOU THAT FILMMAKER?
WHY THE HECK DOES EVERYONE HERE KNOW ME?!

SALE
BECAUSE YOU'RE FAMOUS.
SALE
CLICK

13 KRKY
LIVE BROADCAST

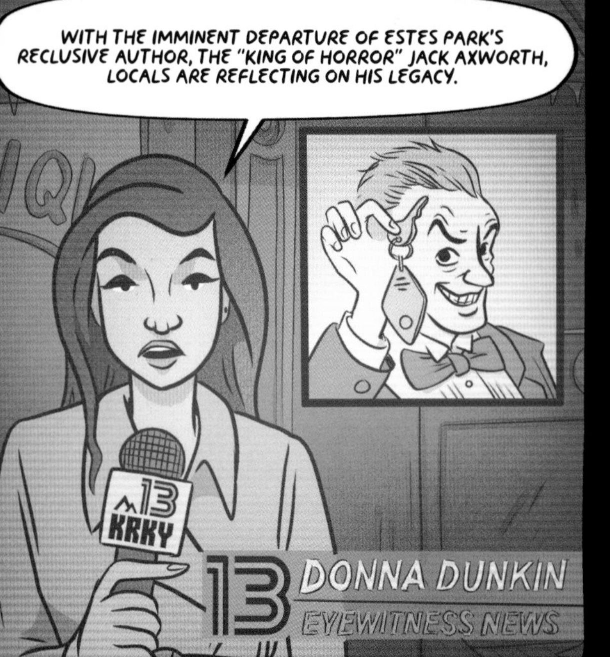
WITH THE IMMINENT DEPARTURE OF ESTES PARK'S RECLUSIVE AUTHOR, THE "KING OF HORROR" JACK AXWORTH, LOCALS ARE REFLECTING ON HIS LEGACY.
13 KRKY
13 DONNA DUNKIN
EYEWITNESS NEWS

I SAY GOOD RIDDANCE; AXWORTH'S A CURSE ON OUR TOWN.

AND HIS BOOKS STINK, TOO.

WITH THIS NEWS, QUESTIONS ARISE ABOUT THE FATE OF THE UNDERLOOK HOTEL, OF WHICH AXWORTH HAS BEEN THE CARETAKER FOR NEARLY FOUR YEARS.
13 KRKY
13 DONNA DUNKIN
EYEWITNESS NEWS

HE USED TO WORK AT THE HOTEL, YOU KNOW.

HOSPITALITY SERVICES.
I WAS A REAL CHARMER.

ONCE A DESTINATION FOR VISITORS FROM ACROSS THE WORLD, THE LUXURY RETREAT HAS STOOD QUIET FOR YEARS. THE SILENCE HAS CAST A SHADOW OVER THE STRUGGLING TOURIST TOWN.

NOT A LOT OF WORK LEFT IN A GHOST TOWN.

13 KRKY
13 DONNA DUNKIN
EYEWITNESS NEWS

'LESS YOUR BUSINESS IS GHOSTS.

BUT THE UNDERLOOK MAY STILL HAVE MORE TO SAY; A YOUNG FILMMAKER NAMED ELIJAH JONES HAS JUST ARRIVED WITH A PERSONAL INVITATION FROM AXWORTH HIMSELF.

13 KRKY
13 DONNA DUNKIN
EYEWITNESS NEWS

HE TALKED ABOUT MOVIES A LOT.

GOOD TIPPER, THOUGH.

MR. JONES IS NOW IN THE UNIQUE POSITION TO INFLUENCE THE MAN WHO HOLDS SWAY OVER THE FUTURE OF ESTES PARK.

I'M DONNA DUNKIN. STAY TUNED TO KRKY 13 FOR MORE ON THIS STORY.
SEE? FAMOUS.
UHHHH.

THE FUTURE OF THE PARK HANGS IN THE BALANCE? WHAT NONSENSE!
CLICK

ELIJAH, YOU NEED TO FORGET ALL OF THAT.
HERE, I'D LIKE YOU TO HOLD THIS CRYSTAL.
WHAT IS IT?

GALENA.
THEY USED TO MINE IT RIGHT HERE IN THE PARK. IT WILL TUNE YOUR FREQUENCY TO OUR QUIET LITTLE TOWN.
MAGICAL!

IT'S NOT MAGIC; IT'S A CONDUCTIVE MINERAL. IT'S PRETTY COMMON IN OLD COMMUNICATION SYSTEMS.
SPIRIT BOX

HERE, PUT THE CRYSTAL BETWEEN THOSE TERMINALS.

WHAT'S THAT SOUND?
THE CRIES OF DEAD MINERS.

UH, WHERE AM I?

RADIO GHOST!
YOUR ONE-STOP PARANORMAL-COMMUNICATIONS SHOP.

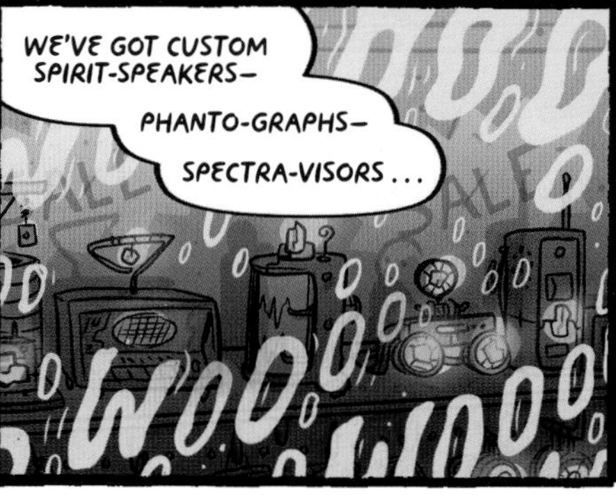
WE'VE GOT CUSTOM SPIRIT-SPEAKERS—
PHANTO-GRAPHS—
SPECTRA-VISORS . . .

NEED AN ASTRAL PROJECTOR?
NO, THANK YOU.

AND TOURISTS BUY THIS STUFF?
WE CALL 'EM UNDERLURKERS.

MOST COLORADO TOURIST TOWNS OFFER FISHING, SKIING, HUNTING—BUT NOT ESTES PARK.
GLOBES

THANKS TO THE "KING OF HORROR"—
WE'VE BECOME AN EPICENTER OF PARANORMAL ACTIVITY.
SO THEY'RE GHOST-HUNTING TOURISTS.
CURSE SITES
RED MOUNTAIN
UNDERLOOK
MT. OLYMPUS
GLACIER CREEK
GLOBES

PARTLY. THERE ARE TWO THINGS THAT LET YOU KNOW YOU'RE TALKING WITH AN UNDERLURKER.
FIRST, THEY'VE GOT AN OBSESSION WITH CUSTOMIZED RECORDING EQUIPMENT.

OH, YOU NOTICED MY ZODAK PRO-MATIC! THAT'S A DAS ZOOM-OBJEKTIV LENS.
IT'S A LIMITED EDITION FROM GERMANY.

SECOND–
THEY'RE OBSESSED WITH JACK AXWORTH'S BOOKS.
JACK AXWORTH
THE UNDERLOOKER
ACTUALLY, THAT'S A FIRST EDITION . . .

HEY!
I'M NOT AN UNDERLURKER!
JACK AXWORTH
THE UNDERLOOKER

LEAVE HIM ALONE, SUZY.
NO JUDGMENT! YOUR KIND KEEP US IN BUSINESS.
OK! I ADMIT HE'S MY FAVORITE WRITER–
BUT I'M NOT OBSESSED.

YOU KNOW, JACK AXWORTH HAS BEEN A TOTAL RECLUSE FOR YEARS.
STILL, IT DOESN'T STOP 'EM FROM SNEAKING UP THERE TO GET A CLOSER LOOK . . .
CULARS
AURAS

AH!
IF I WAS ONE OF YOUR CREEPY UNDERLURKERS, WOULD MR. AXWORTH HAVE INVITED ME HERE? I THINK NOT.

SEE, HE EVEN SENT ME A KEY!
I'M A FILMMAKER—
NOT A GHOST HUNTER.

BUT I STILL THINK YOUR SHOP IS COOL, MS. . . .
THANK YOU. CALL ME EDITH.
I'LL JUST TAKE A SNOW GLOBE, MS. EDITH.

UNDERLOOK HOTEL

SUZY IS A LITTLE OVERWHELMING AT FIRST—
BUT YOU'LL GET USED TO HER BY THE END OF THE WEEK.

DING!

END OF THE WEEK?
SUZY IS STAYING AT THE UNDERLOOK, TOO.

YOU ARE?

I'M TUTORING JACK'S SON, DANNY.
FREQUENCY ENHANCING QUANTUM CRYSTALS
WHOLESALE IN BULK!!
BAGS

DANNY AXWORTH?
THAT'S THE DANNY.
ANCING

OH, WOW.
SO I'LL HAVE A FRIEND?!
WE JUST MET FIVE MINUTES AGO.

I KNOW!
I MAKE FRIENDS REALLY FAST!
FREQUENCY ENHANCING QUANTUM CRYSTALS
GALENA RESTOCK

HEY, SUZY, CAN I INTERVIEW YOU? I WANT TO GET SOME LOCAL FLAVOR FOR MY DOC!

NO WAY. DOCUMENTARIES ALWAYS MAKE LOCALS SEEM TOTALLY WEIRD—
I'LL DO IT!

MOM!
IT'LL BE GOOD FOR BUSINESS!

OH NO!
WHAT?

MY FILM STOCK IS GONE!

IT MUST HAVE FALLEN OUT IN THE CAB!
ZODAK

DON'T PANIC.
WE CARRY FILM.
MISC FILM
GALENA
GLOBE
SOLDER WIRE
AAA+ypical BATTERIES
EXTRA PLANCHETTES
TAROT
SPEAKER

CINE-BRITE, ZOE-SCOPE, BANAVISION . . .
NO, NO, NO.
MY CAMERA ONLY SHOOTS ON ZODAK COLOR FILM!

HOW ABOUT A CUSTOM AURA-MATIC?
SNAP!
IT'S FUN!

HEH.
I'M RUINED.

FLOP.

WHAT'S HIS AURA COLOR?
MAGENTA.

YIKES. THIS IS A DESPERATE SITUATION.
I'M GOING TO HAVE TO GET OUT THE PHANTA-SCOPE.
CLEARANCE

PHANTA . . .
. . . SCOPE?

IT'S AN OLD EXPERIMENT OF MINE. ONLY THING IN THE SHOP THAT SHOOTS ON COLOR MOTION-PICTURE FILM.

IT WAS TOO STRANGE FOR MOST UNDERLURKERS.
BUT THE PARK HAS NO NORMAL CAMERA SHOP, SO YOU DON'T REALLY HAVE A CHOICE.

FOUND IT AT A GARAGE SALE YEARS AGO. IT WAS A WORTHLESS ANTIQUE, SO I ADDED SOME NEW FEATURES.
HM. INTERESTING.

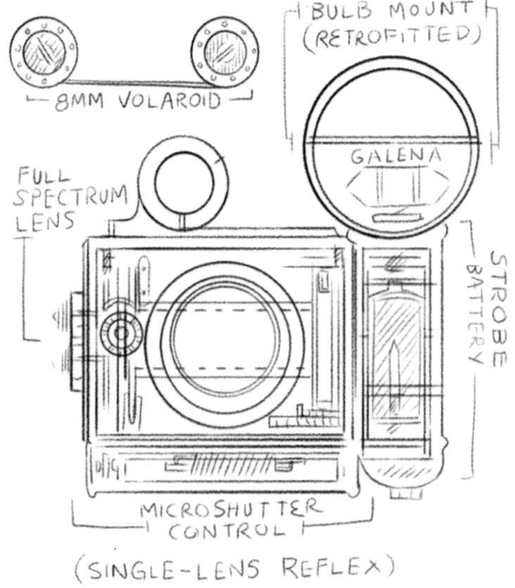
BULB MOUNT (RETROFITTED)
8MM VOLAROID
GALENA
FULL SPECTRUM LENS
STROBE BATTERY
MICROSHUTTER CONTROL
(SINGLE-LENS REFLEX)

WHAT'S WITH THIS STROBE LIGHT?

AH, YOU MEAN MY CUSTOM QUANTUM REALM CRYSTAL FILTER.

IT DETECTS SUPERNATURAL RESIDUE AND OTHER THINGS BEYOND HUMAN PERCEPTION.

THAT'S KINDA SPOOKY.
THAT'S JUST GALENA.
IT'S OUR SECRET INGREDIENT.

THIS CAMERA IS TOTALLY IMPRACTICAL. BUT I'LL TAKE IT.
OF COURSE YOU WILL, UNDERLURKER.

OK, ONE MORE PHOTO.
OH, COME ON.

SNAP!
HOW'S OUR AURA?

MOM, YOU DON'T HAVE TO WORRY ABOUT OUR AURA.
PLUCK
IT'S NOT JUST THAT.

THAT DARN HOTEL HAS ITS WAY OF DECEIVING PEOPLE—AND NOT JUST UNDERLURKERS. I'VE SEEN IT.
GEESH, MOM, YOU'RE SCARING ELIJAH!
NO SHE'S NOT!

I JUST NEED TO KNOW YOU'RE SAFE. CRIPES, EVEN THE UNDERLOOK PHONES HAVE BEEN DOWN FOR YEARS.
FINE! THEN WE'LL BRING A WALKIE.

AND WE'LL CALL IF WE NEED ANYTHING, OK?
HMPH.

I JUST WANT YOU TWO TO WATCH OUT FOR EACH OTHER THIS WEEK, OK?
YOU GOT IT, MS. EDITH.
YOU GOT IT, MOM.

HEY, DAD! YEAH, MY FLIGHT WAS LATE.
YEAH, SHE INSISTED. SHE'S SUPER NICE!
STAYING AT THE HOTEL, TOO!
TUTORING JACK AXWORTH'S SON.
NO, DAD, I WON'T.
OK, I PROMISE.
OK, I'LL PUT HER ON. LOVE YA!

MS. HESS?

MR. JONES, HELLO!
OF COURSE I DON'T MIND! HE'S A GREAT KID.

IT'S ACTUALLY QUITE A THRILL!

SUZY NEVER HAS FRIENDS OVER!
MÜNCHEN
EXAM PREP

UH, HA HA!
PARENTS, RIGHT?!
THEY'RE SO EMBARRASSING.

SOOOO . . . UM, WHAT ARE THESE GIANT TROPHIES FOR?
CIVIL ENGINEERING.
IT'S PRETTY COMPETITIVE.

I'M AWAY AT EVENTS ALMOST EVERY WEEKEND, SO I DON'T REALLY HAVE TIME FOR FRIENDS.
YEAH, I TRAVEL A LOT, TOO.

WHO'S THIS GUY? HE LOOKS IMPORTANT.
THAT'S THE GOVERNOR OF COLORADO.

MY TEAM HAD JUST WON THE STATE CHAMPIONSHIP FOR THE THIRD CONSECUTIVE YEAR.
THAT'S AMAZING, SUZY.

WHERE ARE THE REST OF YOUR TEAMMATES?
OH . . .

STATE OF COLORADO
1876
IT'S JUST ME.

TECHNICALLY, I'M STILL A TEAM.
YOU KNOW, I'M ON EVERY SPORTS TEAM AT BOSTON INTERNATIONAL ACADEMY.

BUT I'M NOT IN ANY OF THE PICTURES. KNOW WHY?
BECAUSE I'M THE ATHLETIC DEPARTMENT'S VIDEOGRAPHER!
HA HA HA!

WHAT I WOULDN'T GIVE TO LIVE IN A BIG EAST-COAST CITY.
I COULD USE SOME REAL COMPETITION.

I GET THAT. BIG CITIES ARE COOL,
BUT IT'S EASY TO GET LOST IN THE CROWD.

MUST BE NICE TO BE, LIKE—
THE ONE, YOU KNOW?

MÜNCHEN
TO HAVE EVERYONE REALLY JUST SEE WHO YOU ARE.

HEY, ELIJAH.
SORRY I HASSLED YOU. I'M JUST SO SICK OF HEARING ABOUT JACK AXWORTH. I CAN'T WAIT TILL HE'S GONE.

IF YOU DON'T LIKE HIM, WHY ARE YOU SPENDING A WEEK AT HIS HOTEL?

FOR THE MONEY. AND I GUESS I'M KINDA CURIOUS WHAT THE FUSS IS ABOUT.
ALL HE EVER DID WAS WRITE A FEW DUMB GHOST STORIES.

SPEAKING OF GHOST STORIES . . .
WHO'S THE GIRL IN THE CAVE?
GIRL IN THE CAVE BY SUZY AGE 4.

GIRL IN THE—
OH GOD.

GIVE ME THAT!
"BY SUZY H, AGE SEVEN."
THIS. IS. ADORABLE.

LOOK! YOU EVEN GOT A GOLD STAR!
WHAT CAN I SAY? I'VE ALWAYS BEEN A WINNER.

WOW.
I HAVEN'T THOUGHT ABOUT THIS STORY IN FOREVER.

IT LOOKS SCARY.

WELL, THE GRAMMAR IS TERRIFYING.

SO, WHAT'S IT ABOUT?

A GIRL DISCOVERS A MAGICAL CAVE...
SHE'S CHALLENGED TO A GAME
WELL, THIS GIRL DISCOVERS A MAGICAL CAVE . . .
. . . AND INSIDE, SHE'S CHALLENGED TO A GAME OF RIDDLES BY AN EVIL SPIRIT.
BY AN EVIL SPIRIT.

USING HER WITS, THE GIRL BEATS THE SPIRIT AND WINS IT'S TREASURE.

WHEN SHE RETURNS TO THE KINGDOM, THE PEOPLE MAKE HER THEIR QUEEN.
THE GIRL BEATS THE SPIRIT, WINS A TREASURE, TAKES IT BACK TO HER KINGDOM, AND THEY MAKE HER THE QUEEN.

HAPPILY EVER AFTER AND ALL THAT NONSENSE.
CAN I READ IT?

I JUST GAVE AWAY THE ENDING.
COME ON!

HAVE AT IT, THEN.
YES!
GIRL IN THE CAVE

YOU KNOW . . .
JACK AXWORTH FAMOUSLY HATES JOURNALISTS AND HORROR FANS.
SO WHY INVITE ME, RIGHT?
I HONESTLY HAVE NO IDEA.

MAYBE YOU ARE THE ONE, HUH?

ALL I DID WAS WRITE HIM A LETTER AND SAY THAT I LIKE HIS BOOKS AND MAKE MOVIES.
THAT WAS A YEAR AGO.

THEN ALL OF A SUDDEN HE INVITES ME TO COME AND INTERVIEW HIM.
I'M THE LUCKIEST KID ON EARTH.

I REALLY CAN'T WAIT TILL HE'S GONE. I'M SO DONE WITH THIS TOWN'S CREEPY MYSTERIES.
UNFORTUNATELY, THEY'RE NOT DONE WITH YOU.

GUESS NOT.

HEY, TURN THE LIGHT OFF WHEN YOU'RE DONE READING.
OK. GOOD NIGHT, SUZY.

ESTES PARK, COLORADO

```
MONDAY-M
Y-MONDAY
AY-MONDA
DAY-MOND
NDAY-MON
ONDAY-MO
MONDAY-M
Y-MONDAY
AY-MONDA
```

COAL MINER'S DAUGHTER
PARK THEATER

TOURS
GOLD

WILD WEST
TOURS
COME ON, ELIJAH!
TAFFY SHOP

WILD WEST
TOURS
TAFFY SHOP

WILD WEST
TOURS
GOOD MORNING!
TAFFY SHOP

HEY, IT'S THE JONES KID!

NED—
GET ME MY MICROPHONE.

UH-OH, DUNKIN SPOTTED ME!
COLORADO

WE HAVE TO GET TO THE FUNICULAR!

IT'S THE ONLY SAFE WAY UP THE MOUNTAIN!
ESTES PARK
COLORADO

THERE'S A NOTE.
WHAT'S THE NOTE SAY?

Use your FUN key to open the door.
RH.

IT'S SOME KIND OF RIDDLE!
FUNICULAR KEY! WEREN'T YOU SENT A KEY?

OH, RIGHT! I KNEW THAT!

235

MINE'S IN MY BACKPACK!
GEESH!

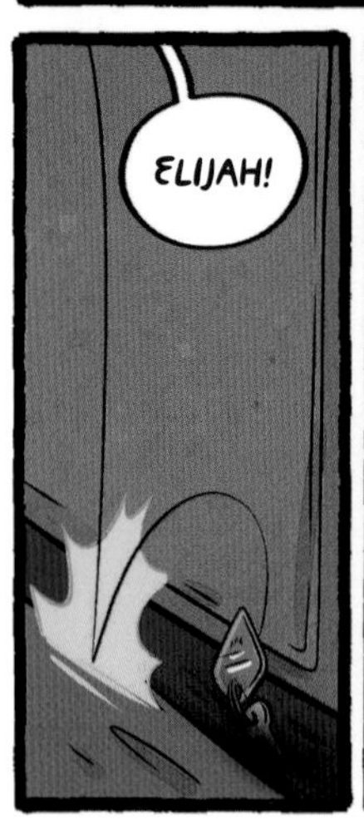
ELIJAH!

EEK, SORRY.

HERE'S MINE!
IS THAT MY BOOK?!

I HAVEN'T FINISHED READING IT.

MR. JONES!
MS. HESS!
SLOW UP, DONNA. THIS CAMERA WEIGHS A TON!

CLICK
UNDERLOOK

HURRY, SUZY!
I AM HURRYING!
THE DRIVE MECHANISM IS RUSTED!

CLANK
GOT IT!

HALCYON MINING Co

CLUNK
DON'T WORRY, THESE OLD STEEL CARS ARE MADE TO LAST 200 YEARS.
HEY, YOU'RE THE ENGINEER.

UNDERLOOK
BOY, IS SHE DESPERATE FOR A STORY.
YEAH, YOU'RE THE BIGGEST THING TO HAPPEN TO THE PARK SINCE THE FLOOD.

YEAH, MY SCHOOL FLOODED ONCE. SOME KIDS PUT A CHERRY BOMB DOWN THE—
NO, I MEAN A REAL FLOOD.
LIKE A YEAR'S WORTH OF RAIN FALLING IN AN HOUR AND THEN FUNNELING THROUGH BIG THOMPSON CANYON, DESTROYING EVERYTHING IN ITS PATH.
OH.
THAT KIND OF FLOOD.
THE DAY STARTED AS COLORADO'S CENTENNIAL ANNIVERSARY . . .
. . . AND ENDED UP BEING THE WORST NATURAL DISASTER IN THE STATE'S HISTORY.
THAT WAS FIVE YEARS AGO THIS JULY.
WE REBUILT, BUT THE TOURISTS NEVER CAME BACK.
WELL, THEY'RE MISSING A GREAT VIEW.
THERE'S ONLY ONE THING PEOPLE COME OUT HERE TO SEE.

THERE YOU ARE, ELIJAH JONES!

YOU GO AND STICK A CAMERA IN A MOUNTAIN GOAT'S FACE—
YOU'RE GONNA GET GORED.
NOTED.

DIDN'T YOU USED TO PLAY BALL AT ESTES PARK HIGH?
THAT'S RIGHT. STOMP 'EM, YETIS.

COME ON, YOU TIRED OLD CAT.

WHAT'S WRONG WITH IT?
SHE JUST NEEDS A PICK-ME-UP. I'LL GET HER PURRING.

ELIJAH, GO IN THE BACK AND GRAB ME THE—
CHARGER.

HEH.
RIGHT ON.

SORRY TO MAKE YOU WAIT, RENA.
EH, I HAD TO MAKE THE ROUNDS ANYWAY.
IT'S NOT JUST WILDLIFE THAT LIKES TO TRESPASS ON THE PROPERTY.

YOU MEAN UNDERLURKERS!

HEH, EXACTLY.
IT'S A HASSLE, BUT WE GOTTA KEEP EVERYTHING LOCKED UP AROUND HERE.

OH, SPEAKING OF KEYS—

OW!
PINCH!

SO, RENA, YOUR DAD WAS ONCE HEAD CHEF AT THE HOTEL, CORRECT?
THE TUTOR DOES HER HOME-WORK!
AND YEAH—
HE RAN THE KITCHEN TILL THE DAY IT CLOSED.
NOW HE HAS HIS OWN RESTAURANT IN DENVER.
I COULDA GONE, BUT COOKING'S NOT REALLY MY THING.
INSTEAD YOU KEPT YOUR JOB AT A CLOSED HOTEL.
NO.
I GOT A PROMOTION.
A PROMOTION TO WHAT?
I GUESS YOU COULD CALL ME . . .
. . . THE CARETAKER.

NOT MUCH OF A PROMOTION, IS IT?

CLUNK!

IT'S SUZY, RIGHT?
HEY, REMEMBER WHEN THE YETIS WENT TO STATE?
P R N D
SNOW-CAT

WE WERE DOWN BY THREE IN THE SEVENTH INNING OF THE FINAL CHAMPIONSHIP GAME.
THAT'S WHEN I STEPPED UP TO THE PLATE.

OH! OH! IS THIS A COME-FROM-BEHIND SPORTS STORY? I LOVE THOSE!

CLICK!
NO, WE LOST. IT WAS BRUTAL.

BUT YOU KNOW WHAT? WE PLAYED THE BEST INNING OF OUR WHOLE SEASON.

I DON'T KNOW SPORTS.
DO THEY GIVE OUT THOSE "NICE TRY" TROPHIES?

NO TROPHY, NO NOTHING.
ALL I'M SAYING IS . . .

. . . SOMETIMES YOU'RE AT YOUR BEST WHEN YOU'VE GOT NOTHING TO LOSE.

I LIKE HER. SHE'S INSPIRATIONAL.
INSPIRATIONAL? SHE JUST CALLED HERSELF A LOSER.

WHOA, IT LOOKS LIKE A POSTCARD IN HERE!
WHAT'D YOU EXPECT?

GIANT COBWEBS, DRAFTY WINDOWS . . .
HA, NOT ON MY WATCH.

OSCAR LEER OPENED THE UNDERLOOK IN 1909.
THERE'S A WHOLE LOT OF HISTORY HERE, AND IT'S ON ME TO MAINTAIN IT.
AH! LOOK AT THIS LOBBY!

IT'S STARTING TO SHOW ITS AGE, THOUGH. EVERY DAY I'M DEALING WITH FRAYED WIRES, LEAKY PIPES—
OH, AND NOT TO MENTION . . .

. . . AN ANGRY OLD BOILER IN THE BASEMENT.

I AGREE WITH ELIJAH. THIS PLACE LOOKS . . .
. . . PRESERVED.

GEE, THANKS.
COME ON, I'LL GET
YOU CHECKED IN.

SUZY?
OK, I'M
COMING.

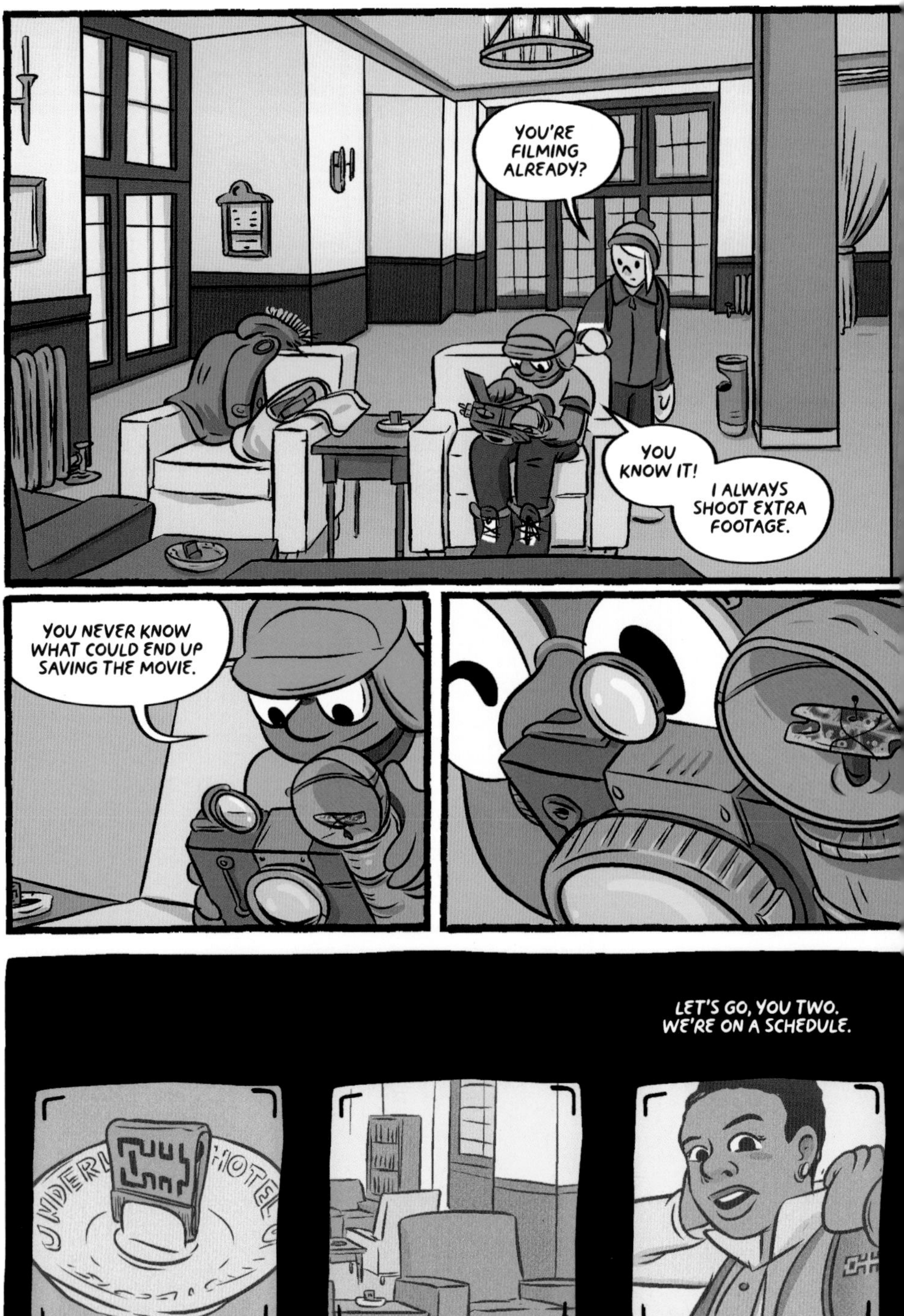

YOU'RE FILMING ALREADY?

YOU KNOW IT!

I ALWAYS SHOOT EXTRA FOOTAGE.

HEY, RENA, DO YOU ACTUALLY GET TO LIVE HERE?
I DO.

YOU MUST GET LONELY.
LONELY?

I HAVE NO TIME TO GET LONELY.

HM?

IS THIS JAPANESE?

HUH? OH, YEAH, EMPEROR HIROHITO LOVED THIS PLACE.

THE HEAD OF THE IMPERIAL FAMILY WAS YOUR LAST GUEST?!

AND HE USED THIS PEN?

AW!

COME ON, IT'S JUST A SOUVENIR!
THIS ISN'T A GIFT SHOP, ELIJAH.

PRIVATE
UNDERLOOK HOTEL
EXACTLY. IT'S A HISTORICAL ARTIFACT. AND I'M ITS CARETAKER.
WELL, TECHNICALLY, JACK AXWORTH IS THE CARETAKER OF THE UNDERLOOK.
WHERE IS MR. AXWORTH, ANYWAY? DOESN'T HE WANT TO MEET ME?
TOURS
TOURS
SKI THE ROCKIES
WILD WEST TOURS

JACK AXWORTH DIDN'T INVITE YOU HERE; I DID.
YOU?!

HE'LL BE DOWN SOON.

BETTER STEP INTO MY OFFICE.

GENERAL MANAGER

THE THING ABOUT A PLACE LIKE THIS–
IT'S NOT DESIGNED TO BE EMPTY.

AS SOON AS THE GUESTS WERE GONE–
IT STARTED TO FALL APART.

NO MATTER HOW HARD I WORK, IT ALL JUST KEEPS GETTING WORSE AND—
RENA?
WHAT ARE WE DOING HERE?

WHERE TO START...
OK, SO WHEN JACK TOOK OVER THE UNDERLOOK, HE TRIED TO MAKE IT WORK. FOR THE SAKE OF THE TOWN, HE TRIED—
EVEN AFTER MY DAD AND THE STAFF LEFT.
I ADMIRED JACK FOR THAT, SO I STAYED ON TO HELP.

IT TOOK SOME TIME TO GET USED TO THE QUIET.
BUT ME AND THE AXWORTH BOYS SETTLED INTO OUR NEW LIFE.
THAT ALL CHANGED A FEW MONTHS AGO...

ONE DAY, I WAS LOOKING FOR JACK IN THE COLORADO ROOM.

AND I SAW SOMETHING I NEVER THOUGHT I'D SEE AGAIN.

Dear Linda,

I must explain to you how all this mistaken idea of denouncing

one of the most perfect days I could have hoped to live.

Love, Jack

I WAS FREAKED OUT WHEN I FOUND THEM, SO I TOOK AWAY HIS TYPEWRITER.
BUT MR. AXWORTH ISN'T OLD ENOUGH TO BE LOSING HIS MEMORY . . .
IS HE?

IT'S CALLED YOUNG-ONSET DEMENTIA. I LOOKED IT UP.
AND IT'S NOT JUST MEMORIES HE'S LOSING.

HELLO
STORE ROOM
IT'S HIS RECOLLECTION OF THINGS WE TAKE FOR GRANTED. LIKE . . .

HELLO
GAME ROOM
. . . WHAT'S BEHIND A CLOSED DOOR IN HIS OWN HOME.

HELLO
JACK'S ROOM
AND IT'S GOTTEN EVEN WORSE.

LAST MONTH I FOUND HIM STANDING OUTSIDE BY THE OLD HEDGE MAZE.

IT WAS THE MIDDLE OF THE NIGHT.

HE WAS BAREFOOT AND IN HIS PAJAMAS.

IF I HADN'T FOUND HIM IN TIME . . .
GEESH, RENA!

I KNOW, I KNOW! I GOT IN OVER MY HEAD.
BUT IT'S GOING TO BE OK NOW.

I WAS ABLE TO TRACK DOWN HIS SISTER WHO LIVES IN MAINE, WHERE JACK GREW UP.
IT TOOK SOME CONVINCING, BUT JACK AGREED TO MOVE IN WITH HER. SHE'S ARRIVING AT THE HOTEL ON SATURDAY.

SO THAT'S WHY JACK AXWORTH IS LEAVING THE UNDERLOOK.

IT'S FOR THE BEST. IT'S NOT SAFE FOR HIM HERE, AND I'M AFRAID HE'S GOING TO PUT DANNY IN DANGER.

HOW CAN I MAKE A DOCUMENTARY ABOUT SOMEONE WHO DOESN'T REMEMBER HIS LIFE?

WELL, UH, THAT'S WHERE IT GETS TRICKY.

YOU'RE NOT HERE TO MAKE A MOVIE ABOUT JACK AXWORTH.

YOU'RE MAKING A MOVIE FOR JACK AXWORTH.
I AM?!

I WOULDN'T HAVE SAID IT SO BLUNTLY, BUT YEAH.

YOU LIED TO ME?!
I'M SORRY, OK!
YOU WOULDN'T HAVE COME IF YOU KNEW THE TRUTH.

DARN RIGHT I WOULDN'T! THIS IS A LOT OF RESPONSIBILITY FOR A KID WITH A CAMERA!
PHANTA-SCOPE.
WHATEVER!

THIS IS BONKERS!

NO, IT'S LOGICAL.
RENA COULDN'T TRUST A PROFESSIONAL FILMMAKER—THEY WOULD LIKELY EXPLOIT THEIR ACCESS TO JACK TO FURTHER THEIR CAREER. AN AMATEUR WAS THE ONLY OTHER OPTION.
I PREFER TO BE CALLED "ASPIRING."

LOOK, ELIJAH. JACK IS NOT A GREAT AUTHOR. HECK, HE'S NOT EVEN A NICE GUY. HE DOESN'T DESERVE TO HAVE HIS STORY TOLD. BUT HE ALSO DOESN'T DESERVE TO LOSE IT. NOT LIKE THIS.

EVERYTHING YOU NEED IS HERE IN THE HOTEL.
JUST FIND THE MEMORIES THAT ARE WORTH SAVING.
THERE'S NOT MUCH I CAN DO IN A WEEK.

A WEEK IS ALL WE HAVE.

OK.

NOW THAT THAT'S SETTLED, IS THERE A SECRET REASON YOU NEED MY HELP?

NO SECRET. YOU'RE THE ONLY ONE WHO RESPONDED TO MY AD.
NOT A LOT OF TUTORS JUMPING TO WORK WITH THE KID FROM THE HAUNTED HOTEL.

THAT EXPLAINS WHY YOU OFFERED DOUBLE MY RATE.

DANNY'S A SMART KID. HE JUST NEEDS TO FINISH THE ENTRANCE EXAM FOR HIS NEW SCHOOL.

I WON'T LET YOU DOWN, RENA. I'M THE BEST TUTOR IN TOWN!
RIGHT ON, SUZY.
OK, I'LL HAVE TO SHOW YOU YOUR ROOMS LATER. IT'S JACK'S BREAKFAST TIME.

MR. AXWORTH?

GENERAL MANAGER
JACK, YOU'RE SUPPOSED TO BE IN THE COLORADO ROOM AT NINE.
DID YOU SEE YOUR NOTE?

THE OFFICE DOOR WAS CLOSED, RENA.
I'M SORRY. IT WON'T HAPPEN AGAIN.

ARE THESE TRESPASSERS?
NO, JACK. I INVITED THEM, REMEMBER?

THE HOTEL IS CLOSED TO GUESTS.
THEY AREN'T GUESTS.

THEY'RE NEW EMPLOYEES.
ELIJAH JONES AND SUZY HESS!
HI.
HELLO.

THEY'RE GOING TO HELP US GET READY FOR THE BIG MOVE.

YOU REMEMBER THE BIG MOVE, RIGHT?

YES, THAT I DO REMEMBER.

IT'S SO COOL TO FINALLY MEET YOU, MR. AXWORTH.
GAH!

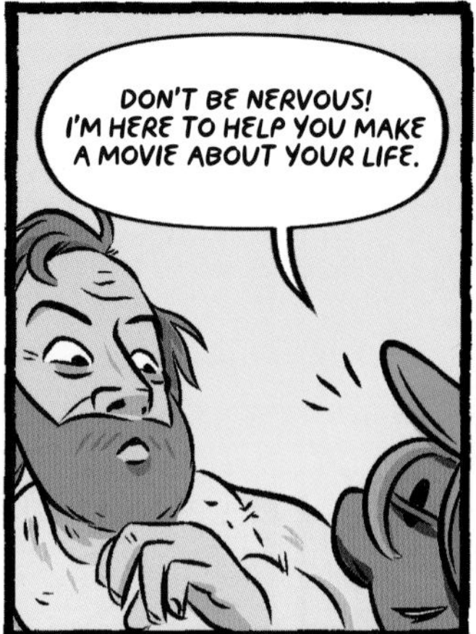
DON'T BE NERVOUS! I'M HERE TO HELP YOU MAKE A MOVIE ABOUT YOUR LIFE.

YOU'RE A KID.
THAT IS TRUE. BUT I'M VERY, VERY ASPIRATIONAL.

DID YOU KNOW I'M A FAMOUS WRITER OF HORROR?
MY BOOKS ARE QUITE SCARY.
YOU'LL BE GLAD TO KNOW I LOVE SCARY STORIES.

ARE YOU ALWAYS THIS . . .
. . . EXCITABLE?
NO, THIS IS A SPECIAL OCCASION.

AND WHO ARE YOU? THE DIRECTOR?
NO. I'M THE TUTOR.

MY TUTOR?!
I'M NOT YOUR TUTOR. I'M . . .

WHOOSH

HA! HA!
DANNY AXWORTH!
GET BACK HERE!

YOU'D BETTER HURRY. IF HE GETS TO THE ELEVATOR, YOU'LL NEVER CATCH HIM.
WHAT?

GO! GO! GO!
OK!

THAT'S WHY I DOUBLED HER RATE.

DANNY!

STOP BEING CHILDISH!

ARE YOU A GHOST?

NO, I'M A TUTOR.

HURRY, TUTOR–
HE'S GETTING AWAY!
FILM
RIP!

CLICK
CLICK
CLICK CLIC
CLICK
DING

HELLO, DANNY. I'M SUZY.
LET'S FIND A PLACE TO TALK.

SKI "76
GAME ROOM
RODEO

I DON'T NEED A TUTOR. I ACE ALL MY TESTS.
YOU CAN ASK RENA.

THUNK
EXAM PREP

AN ENTRANCE EXAM ISN'T JUST A TEST.
EXAM PREP

IT'S MORE LIKE AN ACADEMIC TRACK MEET.
EXAM PREP

OK.

SO WHAT?

SOOOO...
THERE ARE FIVE DISTINCT TESTING SECTIONS.

I'M IN THE MIDDLE OF A GAME!
YOU SURE ARE.

AND I'M YOUR NEW COACH.

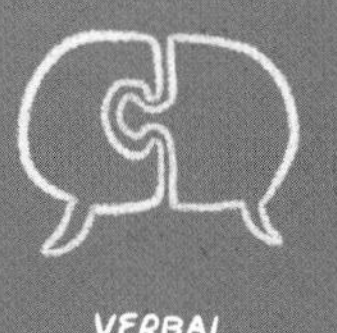
VERBAL REASONING

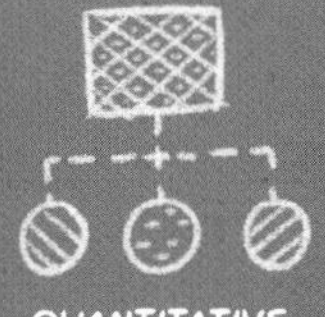
QUANTITATIVE ANALYSIS

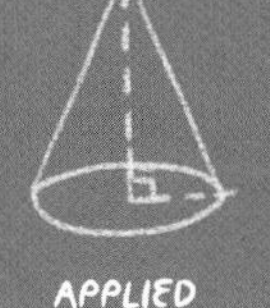
APPLIED MATHEMATICS

READING COMPREHENSION

PERSONAL ESSAY

NOW, I'VE ALREADY REVIEWED YOUR ACADEMIC REPORTS.

WE'LL START BY ASSESSING YOUR WEAK SPOTS AND FOCUS OUR ATTENTION ON—
HEY, SUZY?

HOW OLD ARE YOU?
WHAT?

HOW. OLD. ARE. YOU.
THIRTEEN.

WHAT GRADE IS THAT?
EIGHTH.

I HEARD ON THE NEWS THAT IT'S WINTER BREAK.
WE'RE GETTING OFF TOPIC, DANNY.

BUT DOESN'T A BREAK MEAN YOU KIDS ARE SUPPOSED TO, UM, TAKE A BREAK FROM SCHOOL STUFF?
YOU KIDS, HUH?

YEAH.
WELL, THIS KID IS USING HER BREAK TO EARN MONEY TOWARD SUMMER CAMP.

OH, SUMMER CAMP?! I'VE HEARD ABOUT THOSE! YOU GO SWIMMING AND HAVE CAMPFIRES AND TELL SCARY STORIES AND EAT THOSE S'MORES—
NO, NO, NO.

I GO TO ENGINEERING SUMMER CAMP.

AND IT'S VERY COMPETITIVE. THIS YEAR I'M DEFENDING MY TEAM'S STATE CHAMPIONSHIP.
SO FOR A BREAK FROM SCHOOL, YOU'RE WORKING . . .
. . . TO PAY FOR MORE SCHOOL?

I LIKE LEARNING. I'M GOOD AT IT.
I LIKE IT, TOO! BUT NOT ALL THE TIME.

WHY DON'T I GET A WINTER BREAK LIKE YOU KIDS?

BECAUSE YOU'RE NOT LIKE US KIDS.

EXAM P

AH, HERE IT IS.
NOW, ACCORDING TO YOUR RECORDS, YOU STRUGGLE WITH WRITING. THAT'S ODD FOR THE SON OF AN AUTHOR, ISN'T IT?
I DUNNO.

THE PERSONAL-ESSAY SECTION OF THE EXAM IS A BIG DEAL.
HAVE YOU EVER WRITTEN ABOUT YOURSELF?

YOU MEAN ABOUT MY LIFE?
YES.

WHY WOULD I WANT TO DO THAT?

WHAT ARE YOU DOING, RENA?
STARTING A FIRE.

WITH JACK'S BOOKS?!
HE CALLS IT "CLEANSING."

SAY, WHAT'S THAT YOU GOT, MR. JONES?
OH, UH . . .
JACK AXWORTH

LOOKS LIKE A FIRST EDITION TO ME.

YEAH, THIS WAS MY DAD'S COPY.

I WAS HOPING YOU'D SIGN—
HEY!
GRAB!

NO YOU DON'T!

ELIJAH CAME ALL THIS WAY TO HELP YOU. SO PLAY NICE, JACK.
HMPH.

HE'S BEEN BUYING BACK EVERY COPY HE CAN GET HIS HANDS ON.
JACK AXWORTH

BETTER HOLD ON TO THIS. IT'S ABOUT TO BE ONE OF THE LAST ON EARTH.
WHOA.

I'M SORRY, MR. JONES. I KNOW YOU ARE HERE TO HELP.
IT'S OK. I'VE MOVED A LOT. I KNOW IT'S STRESSFUL.

THERE'S SO MUCH LEFT TO DO.
MANY THINGS TO REMEMBER.
UNDERLOOK HOTEL

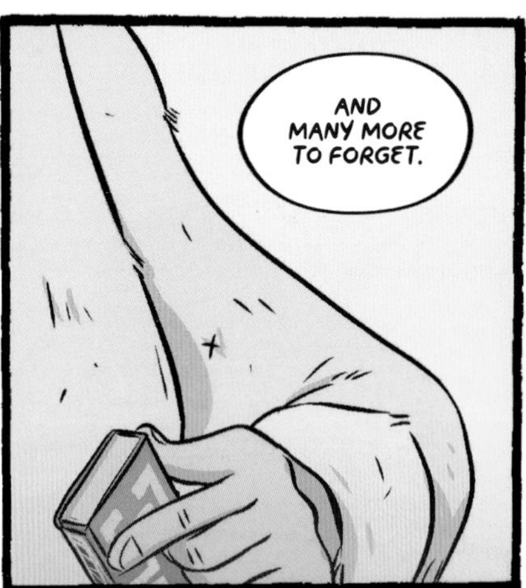
AND MANY MORE TO FORGET.

I THINK IT'S TIME WE GET STARTED.
READY TO ROLL, MR. AXWORTH.

WELL, HELLO,
I SUPPOSE. I AM
JACK AXWORTH.

I AM A WRITER.
I AM QUITE FAMOUS.
I MEAN . . . I WAS.

I BELIEVE THEY HAD
A NAME FOR ME.

YEAH, THEY CALL YOU THE KING OF HORROR.
YOU KNOW, WHEN I WAS WAY TOO YOUNG . . .

JACK AXWORTH
. . . I TRIED TO READ THE UNDERLOOKER! I GOT SO SCARED I HAD TO BURY THE BOOK IN THE BACKYARD! MY DAD WAS SO MAD.

SO YOU UNDERSTAND WHY THEY MUST BE DESTROYED.

NO, IT'S A GOOD MEMORY! PEOPLE LIKE TO BE SCARED . . .

. . . AND YOU'RE THE SCARIEST THERE'S EVER BEEN.

COME ON! YOU LIVE IN THE OH-SO-INFAMOUS UNDERLOOK HOTEL.
DON'T TELL ME YOU HAVE NOTHING TO WRITE ABOUT.

IT'S MY HOME.
I DON'T KNOW WHAT ELSE TO SAY.

TRUST ME, THERE ARE PEOPLE WHO'D LOVE TO KNOW WHAT'S IN YOUR LITTLE HEAD.
WHAT PEOPLE?

PECULIAR PEOPLE.

I DUNNO, SUZY. I'M JUST NOT A WRITER. THAT'S MY DAD'S THING.

ER, WAS MY DAD'S THING.
JACK AXWORTH

OH! UH . . .
DON'T TELL HIM I HAVE THAT, OK?

OOOOH! IS IT AS SCARY AS THEY SAY?
SCARY? NO, I FEEL BAD FOR THE VAMPIRE. HE HAD A HARD LIFE, YOU KNOW?
JACK AXWORTH
THE UNDERLOOKER

WHAT? YOU DIDN'T KNOW THAT IT'S A TRUE STORY?

"A SMALL COLORADO MINING TOWN IS TERRORIZED BY AN ANCIENT BLOODTHIRSTY VAMPIRE."
NOT EXACTLY A BIOGRAPHY, DANNY.

YEAH, BUT DAD'S VAMPIRE IS BASED ON FODOR GLAVA—
AKA THE COLORADO VAMPIRE!

AND HE IS REAL! I CAN PROVE IT.
1906- HALCYON MINERS, ROMERO, GLAVA, OLSEN

THAT'S HIM, RIGHT THERE IN THE MIDDLE!

HELP ME REMEMBER, MR. JONES—WHAT MAKES FOR A GOOD SCARY STORY?
HM . . . IN ONE OF YOUR OLD INTERVIEWS, YOU SAID SOMETHING THAT STUCK WITH ME—
"IT IS NOT THE MONSTER HIDING BEHIND THE DOOR THAT TERRIFIES PEOPLE.
"IT IS WHAT THEY CONJURE IN THEIR MIND—
THE MOMENT BEFORE THAT DOOR OPENS."
I SAID THAT?
PRETTY GOOD, RIGHT?

HEH.
I SOUND SO BRAVE.

YOU KNOW, MR. JONES, THIS CONDITION OF MINE—IT DOESN'T JUST AFFECT MY MEMORY.
IT AFFECTS MY IMAGINATION.

YOU KNOW WHAT I CONJURE WHEN I FIND A CLOSED DOOR?

ABSOLUTELY NOTHING.
AND IT TERRIFIES ME.

YOU KNOW WHY THE VAMPIRE IS BLURRY, DON'T YOU?
'CAUSE SOME OLD CAMERAS HAVE MIRRORS IN THEM.

VAMPIRES DON'T SHOW IN MIRRORS.
I GET IT, DANNY.

YOU DO?!
EVERYONE KNOWS HOW VAMPIRES WORK.

BUT YOU DON'T BELIEVE ME.

WOULD YOU LIKE TO KNOW WHAT I BELIEVE?

ON SATURDAY, YOUR AUNT IS ARRIVING TO TAKE YOU AND YOUR DAD AWAY FROM HERE.

TO A NEW HOME, A NEW SCHOOL, A NEW LIFE.

AND YOU'LL HAVE TO GO, WHETHER YOU'RE READY OR NOT.

I'M NOT AFRAID, YOU KNOW.
PROVE IT, THEN.

WHERE'S THAT PENCIL?

SERVICE VEHICLES ONLY

LET'S HEAR YOU PURR, OLD GIRL.
CLICK! CLICK!

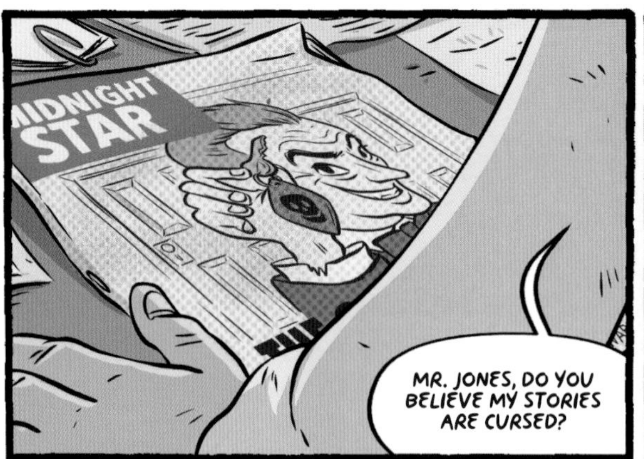

I FEEL LIKE WE'VE JUST BEGUN EXPLORING.

DON'T WORRY, MR. AXWORTH.
WE CAN OPEN MORE DOORS TOMORROW!

BUT I DO WORRY, MR. JONES.
I WORRY SOME OF THESE DOORS CANNOT BE OPENED.

I'LL DO MY BEST, MR. AXWORTH. I PROMISE.

RUMBLE

YES, I'M SURE YOU WILL.

WHAT THE HECK IS THAT?
THAT, MR. JONES, IS MY INSURANCE.

ELIJAH?
WHAT IS THAT SOUND?
UH...

RUMBLE

TUES DAY

TUE SDAY

TU ESDAY

T UESDAY

TU ESDAY

TUE SDAY

TUES DAY

TUESD AY

TUESDA Y

THE QUIET TOWN OF ESTES PARK FINDS ITSELF ALL ABUZZ THIS MORNING . . .
. . . AS A DEMOLITION CREW WAS SEEN PASSING THROUGH DOWNTOWN LAST NIGHT . . .
CLINK
CLINK
LICK
LICK
. . . AND MAKING ITS WAY UP A SERVICE ROAD TO THE UNDERLOOK HOTEL.
CLINK
CLINK
DONNA DUNKIN IS LIVE ON THE SCENE.

WITH CONFIRMATION OF THE HOTEL'S DEMOLITION SET FOR SATURDAY, LOCAL BUSINESS OWNERS HAVE TAKEN TO THE STREETS.

RADIO GHOST

PROTECT OUR HOTEL

13 KRKY

13 DONNA DUNKIN

EYEWITNESS NEWS

THE UNDERLOOK IS THE SOUL OF ESTES PARK!

IT MAY NOT BE MUCH, BUT AXWORTH HAS NO RIGHT TO TAKE IT FROM US.

ACTUALLY, HE DOES, MOM.

YOUR MOM'S GOT SPIRIT.

CONTRACT

PEANUT BUTTER

GRAPE JELLY

HA HA, YEAH. ALL THE LOCAL BUSINESSES DEPEND ON THE UNDERLOOK.

WHAT GOOD IS A GHOST TOWN WITHOUT A HAUNTED HOUSE?

GOOD POINT.

WHO ARE YOU AGAIN?
ELIJAH.
I'M MAKING A MOVIE FOR YOUR DAD.

WHAT'S IT ABOUT?
IT'S ABOUT YOUR DAD.

TO HELP HIM REMEMBER?
I HOPE SO.

ARE YOU GOING TO FILM THE HOTEL GETTING DEMOLISHED?

IF YOUR DAD WANTS ME TO, YEAH, I WILL.
BUT I LIKE YOUR HOUSE. I DON'T WANT TO SEE IT DESTROYED.

HEY, NICE CAMERA.
SINGLE-LENS REFLEX WITH A SECONDARY CRYSTAL MIRROR, NEAT-O.

ACTUALLY, IT'S NOT MINE.
I OWN A ZODAK—

HEY . . .

YOU KNOW THIS CAMERA?

RENA, CAN DAD REALLY TEAR DOWN THE HOTEL?
ACCORDING TO HIS CONTRACT. HE'S BEEN PLANNING IT FOR A WHILE, APPARENTLY.
PEANUT BUTTER
GRAPE JELLY

WHAT ABOUT HIS CONDITION?
WITHOUT A DOCTOR'S DIAGNOSIS, THE CONTRACT STANDS.

BUT WHY DESTROY OUR HOME?
I DON'T GET IT.

HE MUST HAVE AN OFFER ON THE LAND FROM A DEVELOPMENT COMPANY. THIS LOCATION IS WORTH A FORTUNE.

YOU THINK YOU'VE GOT THIS ALL FIGURED OUT DON'T YOU, MR. HOLMES?

BUT I SEE ALL HIS MAIL. HE'S HAD NO CORRESPONDENCE WITH LAND DEVELOPERS.
THIS ISN'T ABOUT MONEY. HE'S HIDING HIS REAL REASON.

HE'S NOT HIDING IT THAT WELL. I HAVE IT ON TAPE.

HE THINKS THE HOTEL IS CURSED.
OF COURSE HE DOES. HE'S JACK AXWORTH.

NO, IT'S LIKE HE REALLY BELIEVES IT. YOU SHOULD LISTEN TO HIM TALK.
NO, THANK YOU.
I WANNA HEAR!

I NEVER SET OUT TO BE THE KING OF HORROR.
THERE WERE OTHER STORIES I WANTED TO TELL.
BUT THE READERS . . .
. . . THEY LIKED THE WAY I LED THEM INTO DARKNESS.

OF COURSE, I HADN'T CREATED IT. THE DARK WAS ALREADY HERE. EACH STORY I WROTE AWOKE ANOTHER–
VERTEX OF EVIL.
AND I SOON FOUND MYSELF TRAPPED AT THE CENTER OF A CURSED, SHADOWY FORM–
WITH NO HOPE OF ESCAPE.

WHAT'S A VORTEX OF EVIL, ELIJAH?
IT MUST BE, LIKE, A WHIRLPOOL OR SOMETHING. SPINNING HIM AROUND AND AROUND INTO A BLACK HOLE OF TOTAL, ABSOLUTE DARKNESS!
GOD. PLEASE SPARE ME THE METAPHORS.
HE SOUNDS SO DEFEATED.

WHAT IF HE BELIEVES THE CURSE IS REAL?
REAL ENOUGH TO DESTROY THE HOTEL?
COME ON.

I'M WITH SUZY ON THIS. EVEN WITH HIS DEMENTIA—
I DON'T THINK JACK IS GULLIBLE ENOUGH TO TRUST A CONSPIRACY-THEORY MAGAZINE.

THE ARTICLE ISN'T ABOUT A CONSPIRACY THEORY. THIS IS ONE OF THE MOST INFAMOUS EVENTS IN FILMMAKING HISTORY.
"KING of HORROR"
JACK AXWORTH
AT THE PEAK OF JACK'S CAREER, THE UNDERLOOKER WAS ONE OF THE BESTSELLING BOOKS IN THE WORLD.

DIRECTOR
ANXIOUS TO CASH IN ON THE BOOK'S POPULARITY, GLOBAL STUDIOS BOUGHT THE FILM RIGHTS AND RUSHED A MOVIE INTO PRODUCTION.

THE TERRIFYING NO. 1 BESTSELLER
THE UNDERLOOKER
NOW A TERRIFYING MOTION PICTURE
SOLD OUT
IT WAS A HUGE SUCCESS. EVERYONE GOT RICH.

AFTER THE MOVIE'S RELEASE, STORIES BEGAN TO SURFACE ABOUT THE HORRORS THAT HAPPENED BEHIND THE SCENES.
THE CINEMATOGRAPHER FOUND UNEXPLAINED CRACKS IN HIS FAVORITE CAMERA LENSES.
THE STUNT ANIMALS BEGAN DISOBEYING THEIR TRAINERS.
THREE SEPARATE PLANES CARRYING CREW MEMBERS WERE STRUCK BY LIGHTNING.
ALL THOSE THINGS REALLY HAPPENED?
THEY SURE DID.
BUT IT GETS WEIRDER.

FOUR ACTORS WERE KILLED ON-SET—
A SET DESIGNED TO LOOK AND FEEL LIKE THE REAL UNDERLOOK HOTEL.

"THE EVIL EVOKED BY JACK AXWORTH'S WORDS WAS SO POWERFUL THAT IT CURSED A WHOLE MOVIE PRODUCTION."
JACK'S REALLY GOT A WAY WITH WORDS, HUH?
IT'S OBVIOUS THIS GLOBAL STUDIOS WAS IGNORING SAFETY PRECAUTIONS AND USING JACK AS A SCAPEGOAT.

PROBABLY. BUT THE MAGAZINE STILL SOLD A TON OF COPIES.
JACK WAS BLACKLISTED IN HOLLYWOOD, AND EVEN HIS PUBLISHER STOPPED PRINTING HIS BOOKS.
I CAN'T BELIEVE PEOPLE BELIEVE THIS JUNK.
COME ON, SUZY. EVERYONE IS SUPERSTITIOUS.

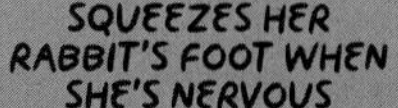

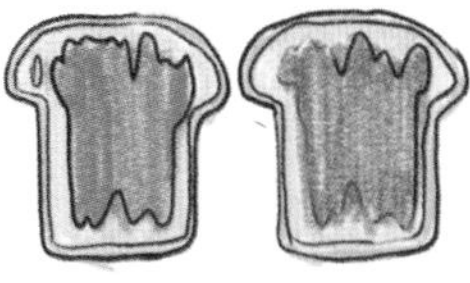

SQUEEZES HER RABBIT'S FOOT WHEN SHE'S NERVOUS

WEARS HIS SHARK! T-SHIRT TO EVERY FILM SHOOT

SPREADS JELLY BEFORE PEANUT BUTTER

ARE YOU ALL LOSING IT?
THIS IS A REAL TRAGEDY EXPLAINED AWAY BY A RIDICULOUS CURSE!

EXACTLY!
PEOPLE WANT PROTECTION FROM THE THINGS THAT SCARE THEM. TO CURE HIS CURSE, JACK NEEDS TO GET RID OF THE HOTEL ONCE AND FOR ALL.

DON'T YOU GET IT, SUZY?! MY DAD IS TRYING TO ESCAPE FROM THE VORTEXES OF EVIL!

LET ME HEAR THAT TAPE AGAIN.
CLICK

AWOKE ANOTHER VERTEX OF EVIL—
AH! THERE! HE'S NOT SAYING "VORTEX." HE'S SAYING "VERTEX."
CLICK

VERTEX, VORTEX.
SAME DIFFERENCE.

ACTUALLY, THERE'S A BIG DIFFERENCE.
VERTEX IS A MATHEMATICAL TERM.

HE MUST BE TALKING ABOUT THE VERTICES OF THE HALCYON TRIANGLE.
THE WHAT?

OH WOW. I THOUGHT YOU WERE A FAN, ELIJAH.

I COULD SHOW YOU ON A MAP, BUT—
OH!

I GOT ONE AT THE AIRPORT GIFT SHOP.

YETI'S MAP!

PERFECT.
YETI'S MAP!

SO, LOOK—
THE UNDERLURKERS HAVE THIS NOTION ABOUT JACK'S BOOKS . . .
GRAPE JELLY
. . . ALL OF THEM ABOUT COLORADO-BOUND SETTLERS WHO ENCOUNTER AN ANCIENT EVIL.
THE FIRST THREE TAKE PLACE AT A SUPERNATURAL HOTSPOT NEAR ESTES PARK.
THREE BOOKS. THREE VERTICES ON A TRIANGLE.
RED MOUNTAIN
CREAKING COFFIN.
UNDERLOOK HOTEL
LAKE ESTES
GARDEN OF THE GODS.
BEAST OF GLACIER CREEK.
GLACIER CREEK
GOLF COURSE
ROCKY
MT. OLYMPUS
BUT WHAT'S A HALCYON?
IT MEANS "GOLDEN DAYS." MAYBE A REFERENCE TO ALCHEMY OR SACRED GEOMETRY . . .
. . . OR THEY THOUGHT IT SOUNDED COOL. I DUNNO.

THE POINT IS: *THE UNDERLOOKER*, JACK'S MOST IMPORTANT BOOK, IS SET RIGHT HERE AT THE HOTEL.

THE CENTER OF THE TRIANGLE.

BLOP

THEY SAY THE HOTEL GIVES THE TRIANGLE ITS POWER—

AND THAT IS THE CURSE JACK IS TRYING TO BREAK.

YOU KNOW, SUZY—

IT DOESN'T MATTER WHAT HE BELIEVES.

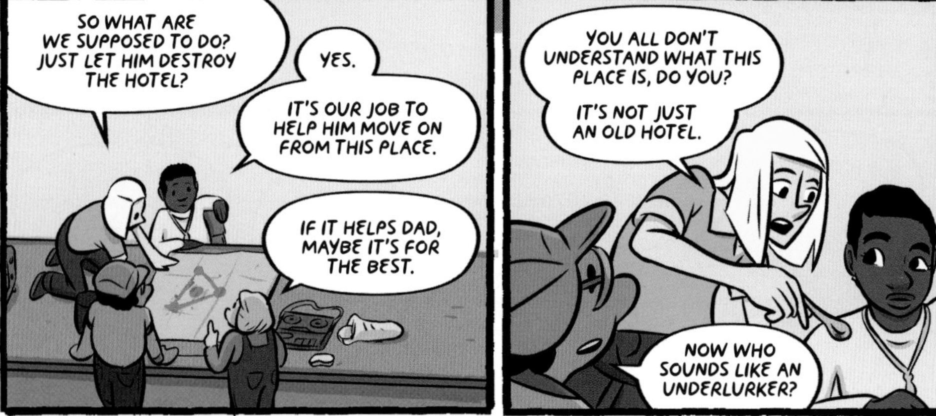

THE HALCYON TRIANGLE GIVES THE UNDERLOOK A PURPOSE.
AN EVIL PURPOSE, BUT A PURPOSE.

IF JACK DESTROYS IT, THE TRIANGLE WEAKENS AND EVENTUALLY DISAPPEARS FROM THE MAP.
AND WHEN IT FADES AWAY, SO WILL THE TOWN OF ESTES PARK.

YOU'RE WRONG, SUZY. PEOPLE WILL COME BACK FOR THE—
THE GREAT VIEW, YEAH? THE FISHING, THE SKIING, YEAH?
SO THAT MEANS YOU'LL BE BACK, RIGHT?

I DIDN'T THINK SO.
FRIEND.

YOU KNOW WHY I'M GOOD AT ENGINEERING?
IT'S NOT 'CAUSE I KNOW HOW TO PUT THINGS TOGETHER.

IT'S 'CAUSE I KNOW HOW THINGS FALL APART.

EXIT
HELLO
ELIJAH'S ROOM
SUZY?

YOU OK?
I'M FINE. JUST GETTING SOME NOTES TOGETHER FOR OUR LESSON TODAY.

DO YOU HATE MY DAD? IT'S OK IF YOU DO. HE'S NOT EASY TO GET ALONG WITH.

I DON'T HATE YOUR DAD. I JUST—
IT'S COMPLICATED.

WHAT'S WITH THE PHOTO?

THIS HOTEL IS OLD.
A LOT OF THE PEOPLE IN THE PHOTOS ARE DEAD.

THAT'S WHY, WHEN I FIRST SAW YOU, I THOUGHT YOU MIGHT BE A GHOST.
OH! THAT'S ME.

DO YOU REMEMBER THAT DAY?
YEAH, I DO.
IT WAS THE DAY OF THE CENTENNIAL PARTY.

I WANTED TO KNOW: WHY ARE YOU SITTING WITH MY MOM?

BECAUSE YOUR MOM AND MY MOM WERE BEST FRIENDS. THAT'S WHY—

THAT'S WHY SHE ASKED LINDA TO BE MY GODMOTHER.

YOU'RE MY GODSISTER?
TECHNICALLY.

OOF.

WHY DIDN'T YOU TELL ME BEFORE?

THE TIME BEFORE THE FLOOD—
IT FEELS LIKE A FAIRY TALE.

I DIDN'T THINK IT MATTERED ANYMORE.
IT MATTERS TO ME.

LOOKS LIKE IT STILL MATTERS TO YOU, TOO, SUZY.

HM. MAYBE.

SO—
WHAT'S WITH THE BOX?

YEAH, THE BOX—
AH, WE WERE DISCUSSING WHAT YOU SAID—
AND, UM, RENA?

WELL, IT JUST SO HAPPENS JACK'S BEEN GETTING A LOT OF MAIL LATELY . . .
. . . FROM PEOPLE WHO SHARE YOUR PARTICULAR CONCERN.

REALLY?
WHAT KIND OF PEOPLE?

PEOPLE WHO, UH, ARE INVESTED IN THE HOTEL'S HISTORY.
PEOPLE LIKE YOU.

HOLD ON . . .
THIS MAIL ISN'T FROM PEOPLE—

IT'S FROM UNDERLURKERS.

THAT'S TRUE.
AND NORMALLY THIS KIND OF MAIL GOES RIGHT INTO THE BOILER.
BUT YOU GOT ME THINKING, SUZY . . .
OOOH, CREEPY!

WHO BELIEVES IN THE POWER OF THIS PLACE MORE THAN THESE WEIRDOS?

AND WHAT IF ONE OF THEM CAN CONVINCE JACK THE UNDERLOOK IS WORTH SAVING.

YOU WANT TO TRUST THE FUTURE OF THE UNDERLOOK TO AN UNDERLURKER?!
ME? NO WAY. THAT'S WHERE YOU COME IN.

IF YOU'RE SUGGESTING THAT I UNDERSTAND THESE WEIRDOS, YOU'RE WRONG. I DO NOT.
SHE'S RIGHT, RENA. UNDERLURKERS ARE BATTY. I MEAN, WHO MAILS SOMEONE A CREEPY OLD KNIFE?

ACTUALLY, THIS IS A PAGAN CEREMONIAL BLADE— A SYMBOL OF REVERENCE FOR THE SPIRIT WORLD.
IT'S A DEEPLY RESPECTFUL GIFT.

HA!
SEE? YOU ARE AN EXPERT!
NOW THAT WAS CRUEL.

SUZY, WE JUST WANT TO HELP.
BUT YOU HAVE TO WEED OUT THE WEIRDOS.

FINE. BUT THEN WHAT? JACK ISN'T JUST GOING TO INVITE THEM OVER FOR DINNER.
ELIJAH HAS A PLAN FOR THAT.

WHEN WE FIND A POTENTIAL INVESTOR, WE SET UP A MEETING WITH THEM IN TOWN . . .
. . . AND I FILM THEIR PROPOSAL.

THEN DAD JUST HAS TO WATCH IT.
VIDEO PROPOSALS? HUH. PRETTY CLEVER. BUT OF COURSE . . .

. . . THIS THEORETICAL INVESTOR WILL NEED TO BE WEALTHY ENOUGH TO MAKE SUCH AN INVESTMENT . . .

. . . NOT TO MENTION SUPERSTITIOUS ENOUGH TO CONVINCE JACK THEY CAN REMOVE THE CURSE . . .

. . . AND AUDACIOUS ENOUGH TO DECIDE BY SATURDAY MORNING AND HALT THE DEMOLITION.

IMPROBABLE BUT NOT IMPOSSIBLE.
LET'S GET TO WORK.

WOOO! THIS IS GONNA BE SO—
NOT YOU.

YOU HAVE AN ESSAY TO WRITE.

ROOM
CAN I AT LEAST OPEN ONE LITTLE LETTER?
NO.
COME ON, SUZY. DON'T BE DULL.

ELIJAH'S ROOM
JUST ONE LITTLE LETTER, SUZY?
ARE YOU HIS TUTOR, ELIJAH? NO, YOU'RE NOT!

UNDERLOOK HOTEL
235

AXWORTH FAN CLUB
VIA AIR MAIL
JACK AXWORTH
Wonderview Ave.
Estes Park, CO
Jack Axworth
Jack Axworth
Wonderview Ave
Estes Park, CO
SAVOIE
DEVIL'S TOWER
NATIONAL MONUMENT
JACK AXWORTH
WONDERVIEW AVE.
ESTES PARK CO.

Mr. J. Axworth
Wonderview Ave
Estes Park, CO
ack Axworth
Wonderview Ave.
Estes Park
Colorado
PASSED
CEN
OR
Axworth
Wonderview

THANK YOU FOR YOUR TIME, MR. LUTHOR.

BIG HORN DINER
SO WHAT'D YOU THINK, SUZY?
THAT MAN IS PURE EVIL. AND NOT THE GOOD KIND.

ESTES PARK
FINE ANTIQUES
HE OWNS A CASINO IN LAS VEGAS!
HE MUST HAVE THE MONEY TO SAVE A DOZEN UNDERLOOK HOTELS.
HE DOESN'T CARE ABOUT THE HOTEL. HE WANTS THE LAND. BEFORE WE KNOW IT, HE'LL BE BUILDING A CONVENTION CENTER OR CORPORATE RESORT OR EVEN AN AIRPORT.

TRUST ME, THAT IS NO UNDERLURKER.

OK, WHO'S NEXT? WE NEED TO GET BACK BEFORE JACK FIGURES OUT WHAT WE'RE UP TO.
DON'T WORRY, DANNY'S TAKING CARE OF IT.

GO FISH, DAD.
WHAT?

OUR NEXT MEETING IS WITH A LOCAL NAMED JANN BADCLIFFE. NOW THIS IS HOPEFUL—
HER LETTER SAYS HER MEMORIES OF THE UNDERLOOK INSPIRED HER FORTUNE 500 COMPANY.

APPARENTLY SHE'S THE CEO OF COOKIE CASTLE.
I LOVE COOKIE CASTLE!

RICH AND NOSTALGIC—GREAT COMBINATION.

GHOST TOURS
OPEN
WILD WEST TOURS
LET'S HOPE SHE'S SENSIBLE, TOO—
WE'RE MEETING AT HER HOUSE.
TAXI!

TAXI
HELLO AGAIN!
HEY, MOVIE KID. WHERE TO?

NINETEEN AVALON DRIVE.

19
AVALON
DRIVE

I CAN SEE WHY MR. AXWORTH WOULD SEND YOU TO NEGOTIATE WITH ME.

WHAT A CUTE CREW Y'ALL ARE!

YEAH, JACK SURE TRUSTS US.

AW, I'M SURE Y'ALL LOVE HIS HOTEL.
HEH, I MEAN, WHO DOESN'T?
RIP

YOU KNOW, WHEN I WAS A GIRL . . .
FILM
ELIJAH! GET OUT THE CAMERA. SHE'S ABOUT TO START REMINISCING.

. . . MY PA WOULD LET ME PICK OUT WHERE WE'D GO ON VACATION.
"ANYWHERE YOUR HEART DESIRES," HE'D SAY.
AND MY HEART WOULD ALWAYS SAY, "THE UNDERLOOK."

WHEN I GREW UP, I LEFT TEXAS AN' BUILT THIS HOUSE FOR MYSELF.

NEVER IMAGINED I'D LIVE TO SEE ITS LIGHT FADE OUT.

DOES IT SHINE FOR YOU?
WHAT, THE BOILER?

NO, THE UNDERLOOK.

WELL, I THINK IF YOU REVIEW THE RECORDS YOU'LL FIND POTENTIAL.
I DON'T CARE ABOUT RECORDS.

THE ONLY THING I WANT TO KNOW IS IF THE OLD HOTEL STILL SHINES.
LIKE IT DID WHEN I WAS A GIRL.

SHRUG

IT'S A SIMPLE QUESTION, DEAR.

ARE YOU HERE TO SELL ME A BRIGHT FUTURE?
OR THE LAST SPECK OF LIGHT FROM A LONG-DEAD STAR?

CRUNCH
CRUNCH
CRUNCH
CRUNCH
CRUNCH
WILL YOU STOP CRUNCHING?
I CAN'T THINK STRAIGHT!

COOKIE CASTLE
CURSED WITH FUN!

SUZY–
FORGET ABOUT THE COOKIE LADY.

BUT SHE'S RIGHT. THEY'RE ALL RIGHT!
NO MATTER HOW I DO THE MATH, THE HOTEL IS A HORRIBLE INVESTMENT.

WUMP

CRUNCH
ANY REASONABLE PERSON WOULD BULLDOZE IT AND START OVER.
THEN WE FIND SOMEONE UNREASONABLE.

YOU KNOW THEY'RE OUT THERE.
WE JUST HAVE TO KEEP LOOKING.

ESTES PARK, COLORADO

```
:::       :::                                                                                                          :::   :::
:+:       :+:                                                                                                          :+:   :+:
+:+       +:+                                                                                                           +:+ +:+
+#+  +:+  +#+                                                                                                            +#++:
+#+ +#+#+ +#+                                                                                                             +#+
 #+#+# #+#+#                                                                                                              #+#
  ###   ###                                                                                                               ###


                 ::::::::::                                                                                 :::
:+:       :+:    :+:                                                                                  :+: :+:      :+:   :+:
+:+       +:+    +:+                                                                                 +:+   +:+      +:+ +:+
+#+  +:+  +#+    +#++:++#                                                                           +#++:++#++:       +#++:
+#+ +#+#+ +#+    +#+                                                                                +#+     +#+        +#+
 #+#+# #+#+#     #+#                                                                                #+#     #+#        #+#
                 ##########                                                                         ###     ###


                                ::::::::                                                  ::::::::
:+:       :+:                  :+:    :+:                                                :+:    :+:                   :+:   :+:
+:+       +:+                  +:+    +:+                                                +:+    +:+                    +:+ +:+
+#+  +:+  +#+                  +#+    +:+                                                +#+    +:+                     +#++:
+#+ +#+#+ +#+                  +#+    +#+                                                +#+    +#+                      +#+
 #+#+# #+#+#                   #+#    #+#                                                #+#    #+#                      #+#
                               #########                                                 #########


                                              ::::    :::                 ::::::::
                                              :+:+:   :+:                :+:    :+:
+:+       +:+                                 :+:+:+  +:+                +:+                                            +:+ +:+
+#+  +:+  +#+                                 +#+ +:+ +#+                +#++:++#++                                       +#++:
                                              +#+  +#+#+#                       +#+
                                              #+#   #+#+#                #+#    #+#
                                              ###    ####                 ########


                                                             ::::::::::
                                                             :+:
                                                             +:+
+#+  +:+  +#+                                                +#++:++#                                                 +#++:
                                                             +#+
                                                             #+#
                                                             ##########


                                              ::::    :::                 ::::::::
                                              :+:+:   :+:                :+:    :+:
+:+       +:+                                 :+:+:+  +:+                +:+                                            +:+ +:+
+#+  +:+  +#+                                 +#+ +:+ +#+                +#++:++#++                                       +#++:
                                              +#+  +#+#+#                       +#+
                                              #+#   #+#+#                #+#    #+#
                                              ###    ####                 ########


                                ::::::::                                                  ::::::::
:+:       :+:                  :+:    :+:                                                :+:    :+:                   :+:   :+:
+:+       +:+                  +:+    +:+                                                +:+    +:+                    +:+ +:+
+#+  +:+  +#+                  +#+    +:+                                                +#+    +:+                     +#++:
+#+ +#+#+ +#+                  +#+    +#+                                                +#+    +#+                      +#+
 #+#+# #+#+#                   #+#    #+#                                                #+#    #+#                      #+#
                               #########                                                 #########


                 ::::::::::                                                                                 :::
:+:       :+:    :+:                                                                                  :+: :+:      :+:   :+:
+:+       +:+    +:+                                                                                 +:+   +:+      +:+ +:+
+#+  +:+  +#+    +#++:++#                                                                           +#++:++#++:       +#++:
+#+ +#+#+ +#+    +#+                                                                                +#+     +#+        +#+
 #+#+# #+#+#     #+#                                                                                #+#     #+#        #+#
                 ##########                                                                         ###     ###


:::       :::                                                                                                          :::   :::
:+:       :+:                                                                                                          :+:   :+:
+:+       +:+                                                                                                           +:+ +:+
+#+  +:+  +#+                                                                                                            +#++:
+#+ +#+#+ +#+                                                                                                             +#+
 #+#+# #+#+#                                                                                                              #+#
  ###   ###                                                                                                               ###
```

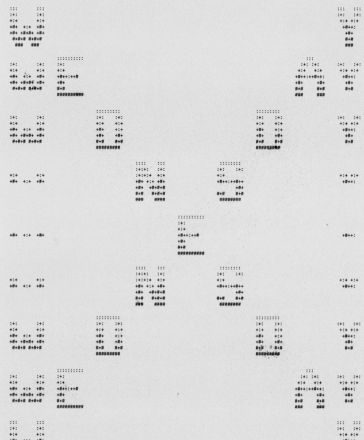

GOOD MORNING, TUTOR.
OR SHOULD I CALL YOU GOD-DAUGHTER?
DANNY TOLD YOU, I ASSUME?

HE DID.
I WAS HOPING THAT BEFORE YOU STARTED YOUR DAY, YOU'D HELP ME RECLAIM A MEMORY OF OUR TIME TOGETHER.

OK.
MAKE IT QUICK.

DID YOU AND I EVER WALK THE LABYRINTH TOGETHER?
YOU MEAN THE OLD HEDGE MAZE?

NOT A MAZE— A LABYRINTH.
SAME DIFFERENCE.

NO.

A MAZE IS A LOGIC PUZZLE. A LABYRINTH IS SIMPLY A PATH; IT HAS NO SOLUTION.
THEN WHAT'S THE POINT?

THE POINT IS TO WANDER.

NO. WE NEVER WANDERED TOGETHER.

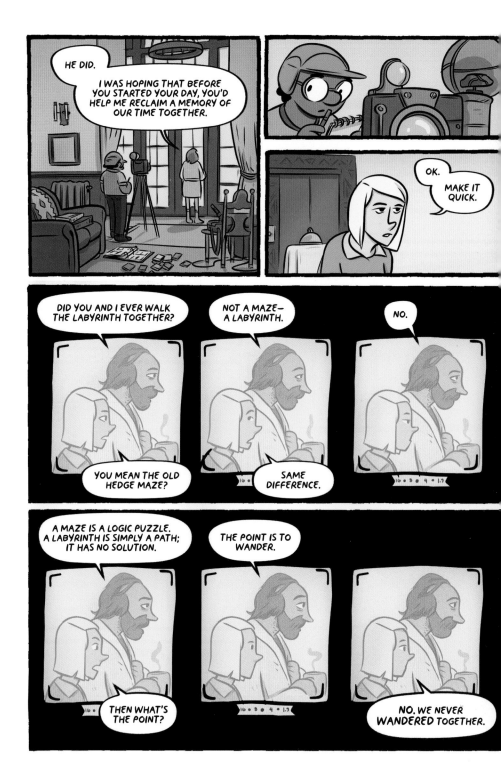

SORRY. I DON'T HAVE TIME FOR THIS.

LET ME SAVE YOU SOME FILM, ELIJAH.

THERE ARE ONLY TWO THINGS THAT I REMEMBER ABOUT JACK AXWORTH—

THE BACK OF HIS HEAD AND THE CLACK OF HIS TYPEWRITER.

I'D LIKE TO CHANGE THAT IF I COULD.
YOU SAY THAT NOW, MR. AXWORTH.

BUT IT DIDN'T BOTHER YOU BACK THEN.

AND IT SURE WON'T BOTHER YOU TOMORROW.

THANK GOD! I'M STARVING.

HOW'S IT GOING?
JUST FINISHED SORTING THE LATEST BATCH OF PROPOSAL LETTERS.

EI
WI RDER
WEIRDEST
TOO WEIRD
AND IT'S NOT IDEAL.

SUZY, I WANT TO LOOK AT THE LETTERS, TOO.
NOT UNTIL YOU FINISH YOUR ESSAY.

AND STOP EATING THOSE COOKIES.
HERE, HAVE A SANDWICH.

HOW AM I SUPPOSED TO WRITE ABOUT MYSELF . . .

. . . WHEN MY LIFE IS SO BORING!
SHH, DANNY! DUNKIN'S ON!
WITH THE DESTRUCTION OF THE UNDERLOOK ONLY DAYS AWAY, HORROR FANS AND PARANORMAL EXPERTS ARE FLOCKING TO ESTES PARK TO TAKE ONE LAST LOOK AT THE ICONIC HOTEL.
THE ATTENTION HAS SPARKED A DEBATE AROUND WHAT IS KNOWN AS THE HALCYON TRIANGLE THEORY.
TODAY, I HAVE IN THE STUDIO DR. STANLEY RUBRIK.
HE IS THE PARANORMAL INVESTIGATOR BEHIND THE BESTSELLER–
SHINE A LIGHT: EXPELLING THE HAUNTS OF THE WORLD.
HELLO.
DR. RUBRIK IS HERE TO HELP US UNDERSTAND ESTES PARK'S UNIQUE SUPERNATURAL PHENOMENA . . .
HEY, I'VE HEARD OF THIS GUY. MOM HAS HIS BOOK.
RUBRIK. HM, NAME'S FAMILIAR . . .

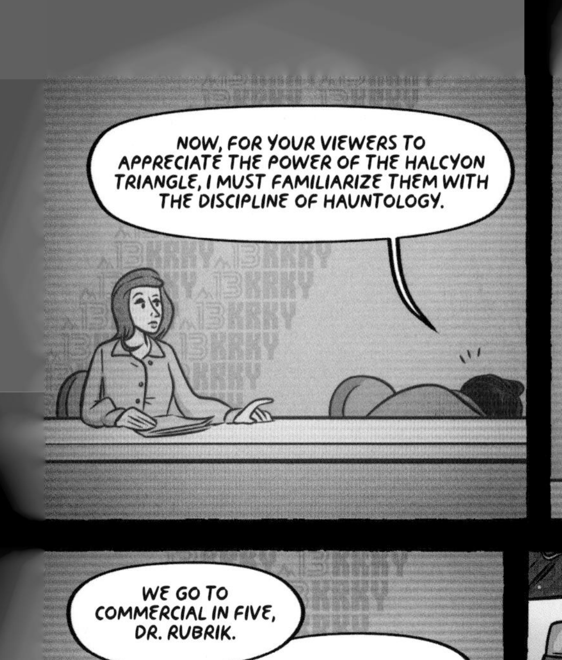
NOW, FOR YOUR VIEWERS TO APPRECIATE THE POWER OF THE HALCYON TRIANGLE, I MUST FAMILIARIZE THEM WITH THE DISCIPLINE OF HAUNTOLOGY.
13 KRKY

WE'LL START WITH BASIC CONJURING TEXTS, THEN MOVE TO THIS GRIMOIRE OF FUNDAMENTAL DEMONOLOGY . . .
MAGICK

WE GO TO COMMERCIAL IN FIVE, DR. RUBRIK.
HM. IN THAT CASE, I WILL NEED TO USE YOUR WEATHER MAP AS A METAPHOR.

NED, LET'S GO TO CAMERA TWO.

A CURSE SUCH AS THE HALCYON TRIANGLE IS MUCH LIKE A STORM SYSTEM; IT CAN OCCUR ONLY UNDER HIGHLY OPTIMAL CONDITIONS—
WEATHER STATION 13

THE MOST IMPORTANT OF WHICH IS LOCATION.
THE CURSE REQUIRES A LOCALE THAT IS—HOW BEST TO PUT THIS—"OUT OF JOINT" WITH THE WORLD AROUND IT.
ESTES PARK

ESTES PARK, A TOWN DEPRIVED OF MODERNITY, IS IDEAL.
"DEPRIVED OF MODERNITY."
THIS GUY IS MAKING WORDS OUT OF MY FEELINGS! HA HA!
THE MORE ISOLATED THE PLACE, THE MORE UNSTABLE ITS ATMOSPHERE.
UNDER THESE CONDITIONS, THE CURSE BEGINS TO ACCUMULATE.
IT CENTERS ITSELF OVER A SYMBOL OF THE TOWN'S COLLECTIVE DREAD—IN THIS CASE, THE UNDERLOOK HOTEL.
WHAT IS HE GETTING AT?
WHAT MAKES THIS PARTICULAR CURSE SO SINISTER IS THE CULMINATION OF THREE TRAGIC ELEMENTS.
THE DEATH OF LINDA LEER.
THE VEXING OF JACK AXWORTH.
ESTES PARK
THE FLOODING OF BIG THOMPSON RIVER.
THREE TRAGEDIES.
THREE VERTICES.
HE'S REDEFINED THE TRIANGLE.

VERY INSIGHTFUL, DR. RUBRIK. THANK YOU FOR YOUR TIME.
AFTER THE BREAK, WE WILL TALK WITH SOME SPIRITED LOCALS PLANNING THE BIGGEST PARTY ESTES PARK HAS SEEN IN YEARS.

MR. AXWORTH, IF YOU'RE LISTENING, PLEASE, IT IS IMPERATIVE THAT WE MEET. I'M STAYING AT THE DROWSY MOOSE–
NED! GO TO COMMERCIAL!

SKI
COLORADO

AHA! I KNEW I RECOGNIZED HIS NAME! LISTEN TO THIS:
"MR. AXWORTH, I AM ONCE AGAIN WRITING TO REQUEST AN OPPORTUNITY TO STUDY YOUR UNCANNY HOTEL.

HE'S A GENIUS.

"IF MY SUSPICIONS ARE TRUE, WE DO NOT HAVE MUCH TIME."
WELL, THAT'S OMINOUS.
RENA! THIS IS OUR GUY!

YOU THINK HE'LL WANT TO BUY THE HOTEL?
I DON'T KNOW. BUT HE'S THE ONLY ONE WHO CAN CURE IT.

I TOTALLY AGREE.
LET'S GO!

HA HA.
YOU'RE TOTALLY NOT COMING.

COME ON! I WANT TO HELP!
GET YOUR COAT, DANNY. YOU'RE COMING WITH US.

NO WAY, JACK WOULD KILL US!
IT'S WORTH THE RISK. WE COULD REALLY USE HIM FOR CREDIBILITY.

THAT'S RIGHT! I'M CREDIBLE!
YOU DO NOT LEAVE MY SIDE, GOT IT?
HEY!
WHAT'D I MISS?

GET YOUR COAT, ELIJAH! WE'RE SEEING A HAUNTOLOGIST.

HAUNTOLOGIST?

DID SOMEONE GET SICK?

DROWSY MOOSE
MOTEL
TV
PET FRIENDLY

12
KNOCK
KNOCK
KNOCK

YES?

HELLO, DR. RUBRIK. I'M SUZY HESS. AND THIS IS ELIJAH, RENA, AND DANNY.
WE WANT TO TALK ABOUT THE UNDERLOOK.

DANNY AXWORTH?

HI!

PLEASE COME INSIDE.
THANK YOU.
LEGGO, RENA!

ARCHAEOLOGY
QUANTUM BRIDGES
PROTOPLASM THROUGH THE AGES VOL 1

OOOH, TAXIDERMY! CREEPY.

TAXIDERMY!
TAXIDERMY!
TAXIDERMY!

HA HA, I'M OK!
SAY HELLO TO OUR GUESTS, LENORE.

HELLO TO OUR GUESTS, LENORE.
NICE TO MEET YOU.

DR. RUBRIK, HAVE YOU REALLY CURED 2,499 HAUNTED HOUSES?
SHINE A LIGHT
A LIGHT

IT SHOULD BE A NEAT 2,500, BUT I'VE GONE UNCREDITED FOR A CERTAIN DUTCH COLONIAL ON LONG ISLAND.
HERE'S TO HOPING THE UNDERLOOK CAN ROUND OUT MY RECORD.

HEY DR. R, YOU KNOW, LAST SUMMER ON MARTHA'S VINEYARD I GOT FOOTAGE OF A GHOST SHARK—
I DO NOT INVESTIGATE MARITIME CURSES.

TOO SCARY, HUH?
I HAVE ACUTE SEASICKNESS.

EW.

A 1/96" SCALE MODEL OF THE UNDERLOOK. IMPRESSIVE.
YOU HAVE A KEEN EYE, YOUNG LADY. BUT THIS IS MORE THAN JUST A MODEL . . .

THIS IS THE FUTURE OF PARANORMAL INVESTIGATION.

LOOK, LENORE. IT'S MY HOUSE!
BUT TINY AND CUTE!

BUT WHY REVERSE-ENGINEER THE UNDERLOOK?

AS MY DEAR FRIEND CARL SAGAN ONCE SAID—

"IN A DEMON-HAUNTED WORLD . . .
. . . SCIENCE IS A CANDLE IN THE DARK."

FLICK

IF I AM TO FIND THE SOURCE OF THE CURSE . . .
. . . I MUST ILLUMINATE THE BUILDING'S TRUE NATURE.

AS YOU CAN SEE, IT IS A WORK IN PROGRESS. I WAS ABLE TO REPLICATE THE EXTERIOR FROM PHOTOS . . .
. . . BUT I CAN FIND NO SCHEMATICS OF THE INFRASTRUCTURE.

THAT'S NOT A SURPRISE. THE FOUNDER, OSCAR LEER, LIKED HIS SECRETS.

A SHAME, FOR IT HAS LEFT ME WITH WHAT I FEAR MOST.
WHAT IS THAT?

A PARADOX IN THE HEART OF THE HOTEL.
I FEAR AMBIGUITY ABOVE ALL ELSE.
FOR ME, IT'S FROGS.

HM.

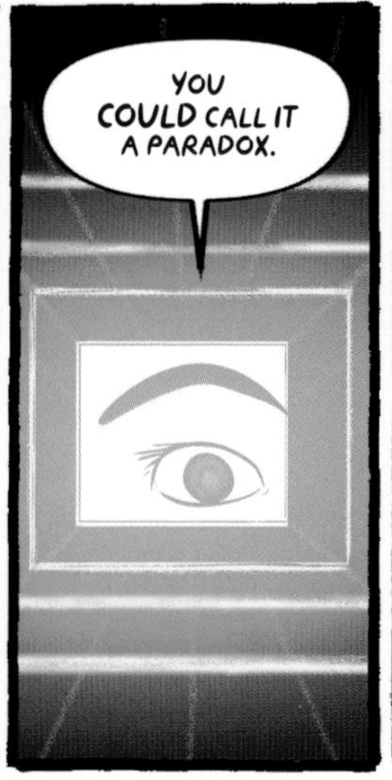
YOU COULD CALL IT A PARADOX.

I CALL IT A MISCALCULATION.

WHERE'S YOUR PROOF?
WHERE'S YOUR PROOF?
WHERE'S YOUR PROOF?

UNDERLOOK HOTEL
FLOOR PLAN
FOR YEARS I'VE BEEN GATHERING PHOTOS, ARTICLES, LETTERS.
YET THE STORY OF THE HOTEL REMAINS INCOMPLETE, DISJOINTED BY TALES OF STRANGE ENCOUNTERS.

UNDERLOOK HOTEL
FLOOR PLAN
IMPOSSIBLE WINDOWS.
HALLWAYS TO NOWHERE.
DOORS WITHOUT ROOMS.
PARADOXES THAT HAUNTED GUESTS, HIDDEN WITHIN THE WALLS OF A CENTURY-OLD HOTEL.
THEIR ACCOUNTS, WHEN COLLECTED, REVEAL A DARKNESS SO PERSISTENT IT PASSES ACROSS HISTORY . . .
. . . WITH THE EASE OF AN AFTERNOON SHADOW CROSSING THE FLOOR.

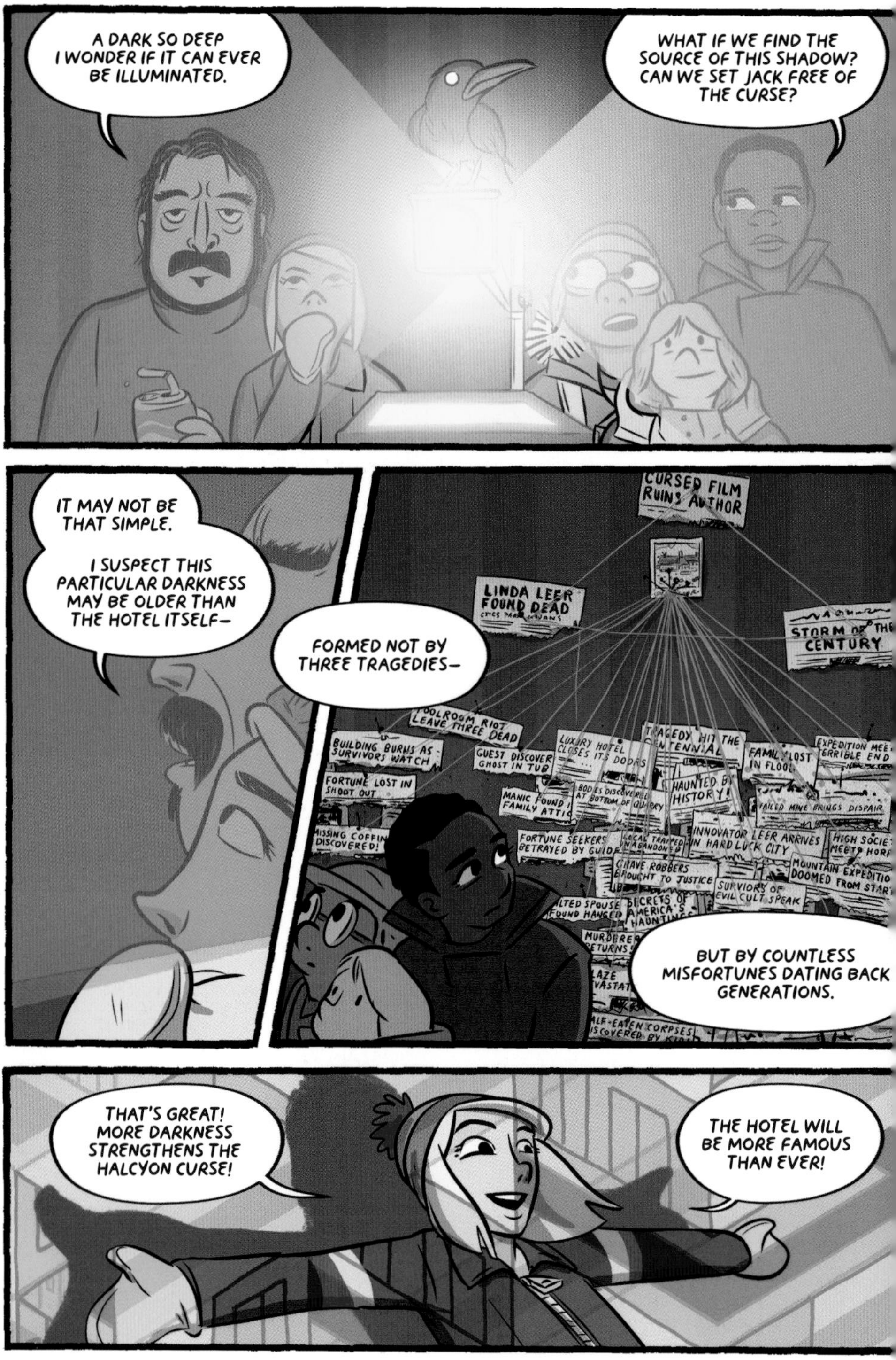

IT MAY NOT BE THAT SIMPLE.

I SUSPECT THIS PARTICULAR DARKNESS MAY BE OLDER THAN THE HOTEL ITSELF—

FORMED NOT BY THREE TRAGEDIES—

CURSED FILM RUINS AUTHOR

LINDA LEER FOUND DEAD

STORM OF THE CENTURY

POOLROOM RIOT LEAVE THREE DEAD

BUILDING BURNS AS SURVIVORS WATCH

GUEST DISCOVERS GHOST IN TUB

LUXURY HOTEL CLOSES ITS DOORS

TRAGEDY HIT THE CENTENNIAL

FAMILY LOST IN FLOOD

FORTUNE LOST IN SHOOT OUT

BODIES DISCOVERED AT BOTTOM OF QUARRY

HAUNTED BY HISTORY!

FAILED MINE BRINGS DISPAIR

MISSING COFFIN DISCOVERED!

FORTUNE SEEKERS BETRAYED BY GUIDE

INNOVATOR LEER ARRIVES IN HARD LUCK CITY

GRAVE ROBBERS BROUGHT TO JUSTICE

MOUNTAIN EXPEDITION DOOMED FROM START

SURVIORS OF EVIL CULT SPEAK

SECRETS OF AMERICA'S HAUNTINGS

BUT BY COUNTLESS MISFORTUNES DATING BACK GENERATIONS.

THAT'S ONE OUTCOME. THERE IS ALSO A CHANCE THE DISCOVERY WILL FURTHER DESTABILIZE THE CURSE AND RAIN DOWN DESPAIR ON ESTES PARK.
AH, RIGHT, YOUR WEATHER METAPHOR. ALMOST FORGOT.

THIS STORM THREATENS EVERYTHING YOU HOLD DEAR.
I MUST BE ALLOWED TO EXPLORE THE HOTEL IMMEDIATELY.

SURE YOU HAVEN'T BEEN THERE ALREADY?

WHAT ARE YOU IMPLYING?
OH, JUST CURIOUS . . . WHERE YOU GOT PHOTOS OF THE INSIDE OF THE HOTEL.

ESTES PARK HISTORICAL SOCIETY.
FUNNY. I HEARD THEIR ARCHIVES WERE DESTROYED IN THE BIG FLOOD.

I'LL BE BLUNT, MR. RUBRIK. YOU REALLY CREEP ME OUT.
I THINK YOU'RE A FRAUD WHO PREYS ON SMALL-TOWN SUPERSTITION.
BUT YOU'RE NOT THE ONE HE NEEDS TO CONVINCE, ARE YOU, RENA?

YOU'RE RIGHT, YOUNG LADY. THE ONLY ONE WHO HOLDS THE FATE OF THE UNDERLOOK HOTEL IS . . .

NOPE.

. . . DANNY AXWORTH.

ME?

WINCHESTER HOUSE (#2497)

FRANKLIN CASTLE (#2498)

FALL RIVER INN (#2499)

BEHIND EVERY FAMOUS HAUNT I'VE ENCOUNTERED WAS A MYSTERY WAITING TO BE SOLVED.

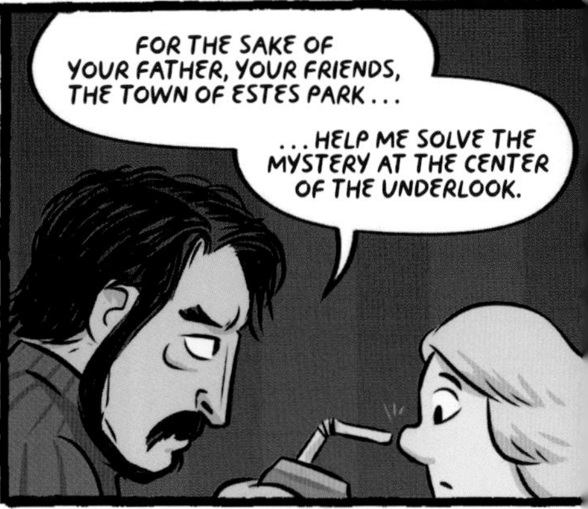
FOR THE SAKE OF YOUR FATHER, YOUR FRIENDS, THE TOWN OF ESTES PARK . . .
. . . HELP ME SOLVE THE MYSTERY AT THE CENTER OF THE UNDERLOOK.

BUT PEOPLE LIKE MYSTERIES, MR. R!
MOM WOULD SAY PEOPLE LIKED OUR HOTEL BECAUSE IT FELT "BIGGER ON THE INSIDE."

WELL, I ADMIT THAT IS MYSTERIOUS!
WHAT DO YOU THINK SHE MEANT BY "BIGGER ON THE INSIDE"?

YOU KNOW, LIKE WITH PEOPLE.

EVEN IF YOU SPEND EVERY DAY WITH SOMEONE–

YOU CAN NEVER KNOW EVERYTHING THAT'S INSIDE THEM.

SHH!

MOM WOULD SAY OUR MYSTERIES MAKE US SPECIAL.

YOUR MOTHER HAD A WAY WITH WORDS.
YEAH, SHE LIKED TO READ.

YOUR DEARLY DEPARTED MOTHER, LINDA LEER, GREAT-GRANDDAUGHTER OF OSCAR LEER—SHE WAS THE RIGHTFUL HEIR TO THE HOTEL . . .
AXWORTH
LEER
. . . AND ITS MYSTERIES.

I DON'T KNOW IF MOM HAD ANSWERS TO THOSE MYSTERIES.
SHE DID HAVE A KEY, THOUGH.

KEY?

I MUST INSPECT THIS KEY.
NOW HOLD ON, DR. RUBRIK. THE DEAL IS YOU TALK TO THE CAMERA, NOT TO DANNY.

DON'T YOU SEE?
THE SECRET LIES WITH LINDA LEER.
1974

SECRET LIES SECRET
SECRET LIES
SECRET LIES SECRET
OK, WE'RE DONE HERE.
IT'S NOT TOO LATE, DANNY BOY. YOU HAVE THE POWER TO SET HER FREE.

SECRET LIES SECRET LIES SECRET LIES
SHUT UP, BIRD!
SET HER FREE?

WE'RE GOING, SUZY
HEY, WAIT A SEC!

RUBRIK, I THINK—

SLAM!

WHAT'S HE MEAN, "SET HER FREE"?
WHERE'S MY MOM, RENA?
JUST A METAPHOR, DANNY.

ALL HE CARES ABOUT ARE GHOST STORIES, JUST LIKE EVERYONE ELSE.

HEY! WE HAVE TO GO BACK AND HELP THE DOCTOR FINISH HIS MODEL . . .

I KNOW YOU'VE GOT A KNACK FOR ENGINEERING, SUZY, BUT YOU SURE AS HECK DON'T UNDERSTAND HOW PEOPLE WORK.

I'M JUST STICKING TO THE PLAN!

SOMETIMES PLANS CHANGE, SUZY.
VACANCY

I KNOW THAT.
DROWSY MOOSE
MOTEL
TV

HEY, SUZY?
HM?

I WANT TO SHOW YOU WHAT MY KEY DOES.

LOOK, DANNY.
I WAS WRONG TO BRING YOU WITH US TODAY.

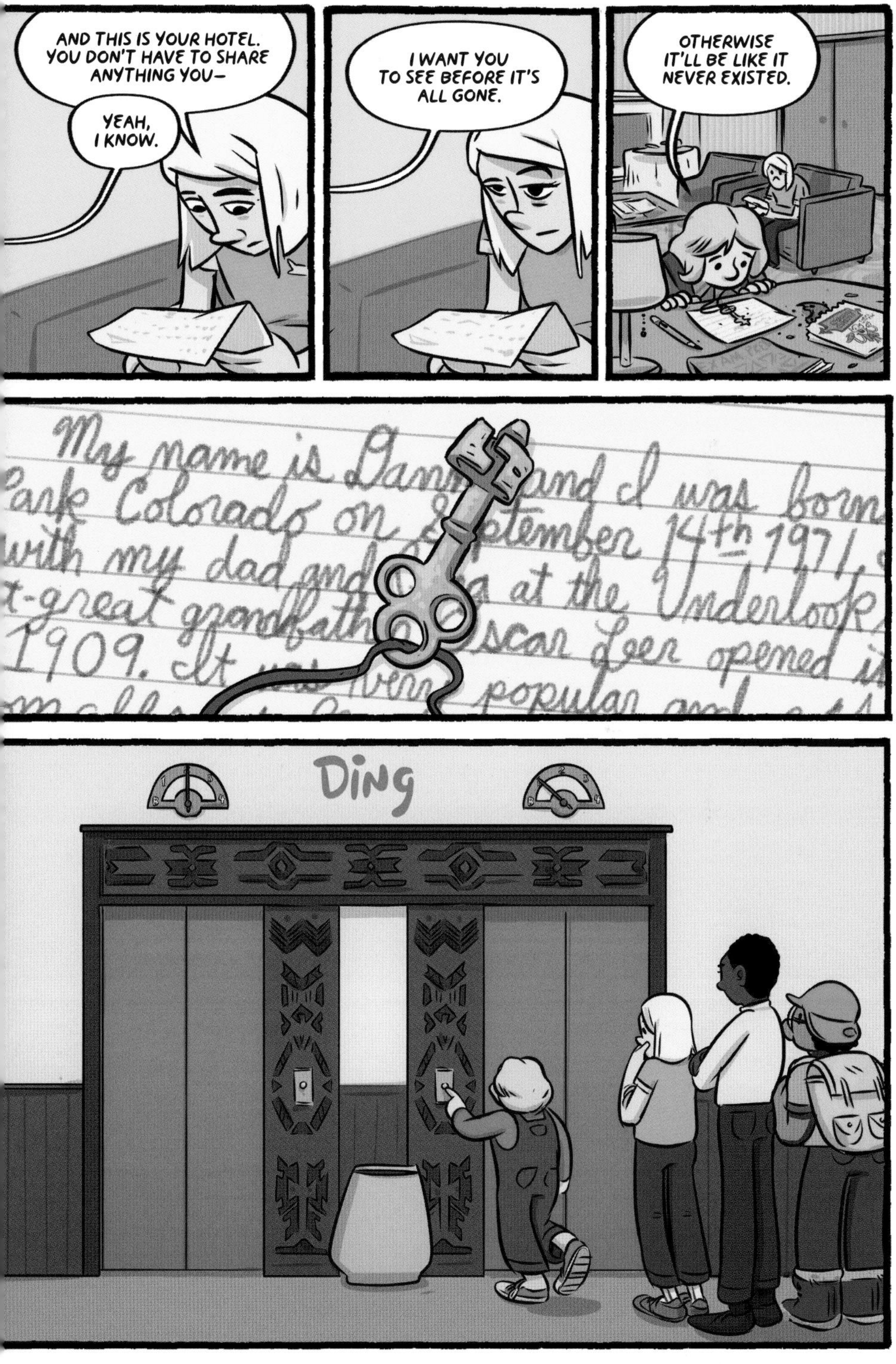

My name is Dann and I was born
ark Colorado on ptember 14th 1971
with my dad and at the Underlook
t-great grandfath scar Leer opened i
1909. It very popular and

DING

READY?

CLANK

CLUNK

HALCYON MINING Co

WHAT?
I SAID READY!

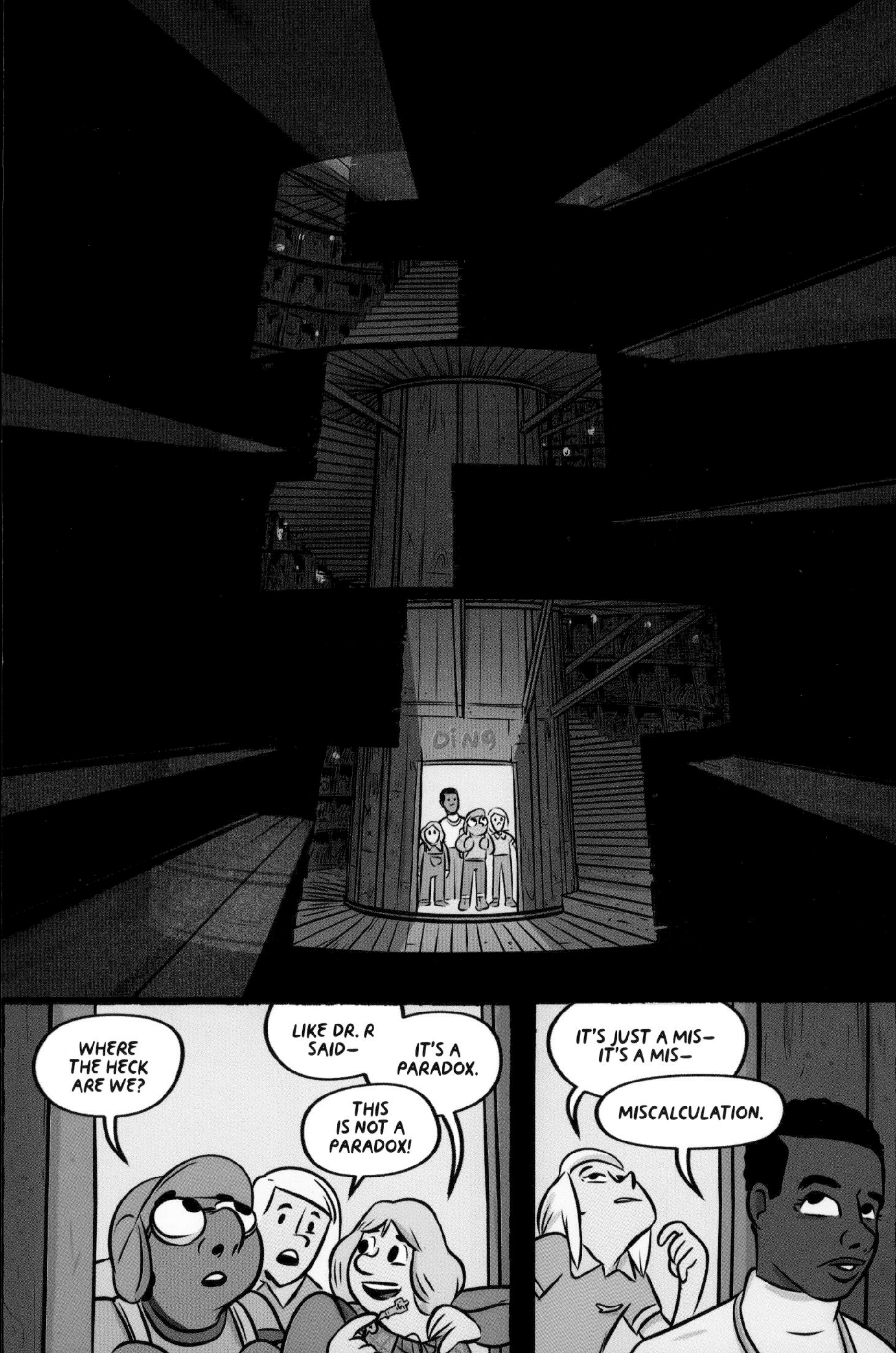
DING
WHERE THE HECK ARE WE?
LIKE DR. R SAID—
IT'S A PARADOX.
THIS IS NOT A PARADOX!
IT'S JUST A MIS— IT'S A MIS—
MISCALCULATION.

DOES YOUR DAD KNOW ABOUT THIS?

NO WAY! ONLY MY KEY OPENS IT.

LOOK AT THIS OLD FILMMAKING EQUIPMENT.

IT'S MY GREAT-GREAT-GRANDPA'S STUFF.

LEER

THAT'S RIGHT. BEFORE BUILDING THE UNDERLOOK, OSCAR LEER MADE HIS FORTUNE SELLING FILM-PROCESSING TECHNOLOGY TO THE ZODAK COMPANY.

LEER

POP!

LEER

SURE! PUT THESE ON YOUR FINGERS. NOW, THERE'S GONNA BE A LITTLE SHOCK . . .
SAY CHEESE!
BZZT
BZZT
BZZT
BZZT
WHOA.
IT'S THE ORIGINAL UNDERLURKER CAMERA.

GREAT-GREAT-GRANDPA USED TO MAKE MOVIES, TOO. THIS IS HIM AND HIS FILM CREW!

WHAT?!
THAT'S THOMAS EDISON STANDING NEXT TO HIM!
YOU MEAN . . . THE LIGHT-BULB GUY?

EDISON STARTED ONE OF THE FIRST MOVIE STUDIOS.
FRANKENSTEIN
1910
Thomas A. Edison
KINETOGRAM

DANNY! YOUR GREAT-GREAT-GRANDPA'S "STUFF" IS A PRICELESS COLLECTION OF AMERICAN FILM HISTORY.
OH.
Sweetheart Tonight my ambition will be accomplished. When I am finished I shall return to claim you as my bride. Your devoted, Frankenstein
TWO YEARS LATER FRANKENSTEIN HAS DISCOVERED THE SECRET OF LIFE
INSTEAD OF A PERFECT HUMAN BEING THE EVIL IN FRANKENSTEIN'S MIND CREATES A MONSTER

OH MY GOD, THIS IS A PRINT OF EDISON'S ADAPTATION OF *FRANKENSTEIN.* DO YOU KNOW HOW RARE THIS IS?
NO.
THEN JACK CAN'T DESTROY IT.
RIGHT! IT'D BE, LIKE, AGAINST THE LAW.

DON'T YOU SEE, DANNY?
THIS IS HOW WE SAVE THE HOTEL!
DANNY, WHY DIDN'T YOU BRING US HERE BEFORE?
BECAUSE–
I PROMISED MY MOM.
HER SICKNESS KEPT HER UP AT NIGHT. I'D HEAR HER WALKING THE HALLS ALONE.
IT SCARED ME AT FIRST, BUT FINALLY I GOT THE COURAGE TO COME OUT OF MY ROOM AND WE'D WALK TOGETHER.

ONE NIGHT, SHE BROUGHT ME HERE.
IT BECAME OUR SECRET SPOT.

AND NOW I NEED TO SHARE IT WITH YOU–
SO SHE DOESN'T GET FORGOTTEN.

SHE'S FAMILY, DANNY. SHE'LL ALWAYS BE WITH YOU.
THAT'S NOT TRUE.
DAD FORGOT HER.

AND SO DID SUZY.

THIS PLACE IS SO COZY. WHAT I WOULDN'T GIVE TO WATCH A MOVIE RIGHT NOW.

WE CAN'T RISK DAMAGING THE FILM!

I KNOW THAT! I'M JUST SAYING IT'D BE NICE.

NO, WHAT YOU COULD USE IS A . . .
. . . MOVIE NIGHT!

Screaming Golden Bonkers!
GLAZED POPCORN SNACK

TALK ABOUT ANTIQUES.

OLD WEIRD MOVIE SNACKS?! I WANT ONE!
SO WHAT DO Y'ALL WANT TO WATCH? WE'VE GOT ALL THE CLASSICS—

HM. I DON'T RECOGNIZE THIS LAST ONE.
OH, THAT'S GIRL IN THE CAVE. IT'S SO SCARY.
GIRL IN THE CAVE?!
CAN I SEE THAT PLEASE?
SUZY, GET UP HERE!
LOOK AT THIS!
THE CAVE ON THIS SLIDE...
THE CAVE IN YOUR BOOK...
THEY HAVE THE SAME SYMBOLS!
GIRL IN THE CAVE

SUZY, ARE YOU THE GIRL IN THE CAVE?!
OF COURSE I'M NOT!
AM I?
WHOA, WHOA, WHOA.
SUZY, YOU WERE LINDA'S GODDAUGHTER, YEAH?
YEAH.
SHE MUST HAVE TOLD YOU THE STORY WHEN YOU WERE LITTLE.
THEN YOU WENT OFF AND MADE YOUR OWN VERSION.
IT'S POSSIBLE...
RENA'S RIGHT. THE STORIES AREN'T THE SAME.
SEE? NOT EVERY COINCIDENCE IS A CONSPIRACY.
IN SUZY'S BOOK, THE GIRL DEFEATS A SHADOW AND CLAIMS THE TREASURE.
HOW DOES YOURS END?
UM...
NOT SO HAPPILY.

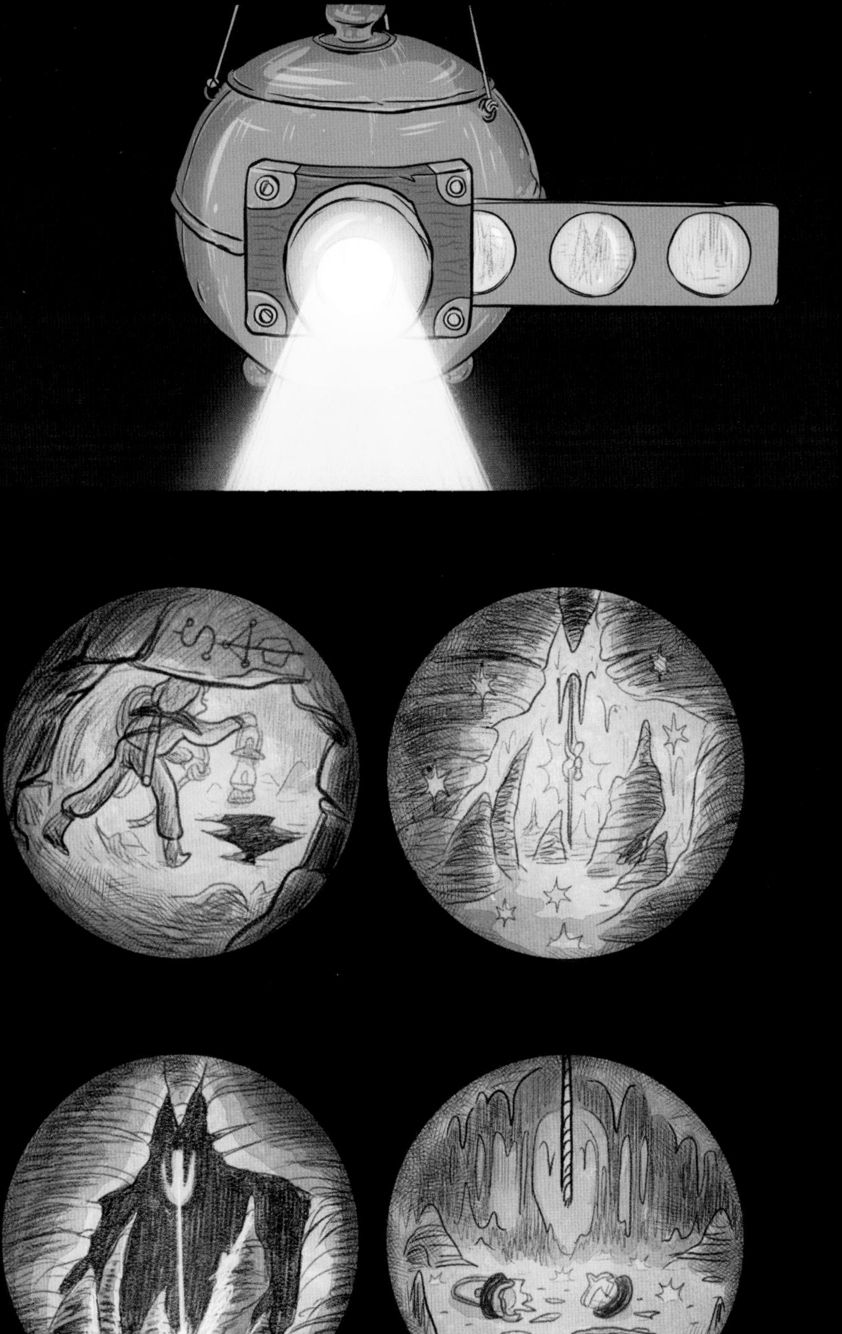

THE UNDERLOOK HOTEL

ESTES PARK, COLORADO

THURSDAY

THURSDAY

THURSDAY

THURSDAY

HELLO
JACK'S BATHROOM
YOU WON'T REGRET THIS, MS. WOODLAND.
PERFECT! SEE YOU THEN!

SUZY! YOU'RE ACTUALLY SMILING!
TELL ME YOU GOT SOMEONE ON THE PHONE?!
THE MUSEUM OF FILM PUT ME IN TOUCH WITH A CURATOR—THIS LADY, ANGELA WOODLAND.
SHE'S SAYS IF LEER'S COLLECTION IS HALF AS GOOD AS WE THINK, HER MUSEUM WILL SUBMIT THE HOTEL TO THE NATIONAL REGISTER OF HISTORIC PLACES!
BEST OF ALL, THERE'S NOTHING JACK AXWORTH CAN DO TO STOP IT.

HELLO ELIJAH'S ROOM
ELIJAH! DANNY!
WAIT TILL YOU HEAR THIS!
UH, WHAT'S WITH YOU TWO?

AH, GOOD.
WE'RE ALL HERE.
JACK?

I'M SORRY TO INTERRUPT . . .
. . . BUT I HAVE LITTLE TIME LEFT HERE, AND THERE IS SOMEONE YOU MUST HELP ME SAY GOODBYE TO.

YA KNOW I KNOW WHO YA ARE.
YES, IT IS TRUE. I AM THE FAMOUS AUTHOR–
AA Bean

AUTHOR? NAH.
YER THE UNDERLOOK GUY. I'VE BEEN SEEING THE NEWS; YA GOT A WEIRD LIFE.

IT'S GONNA MAKE ONE HECK OF A MOVIE, HEY, KID?
AH, YEAH. WE'LL SEE.

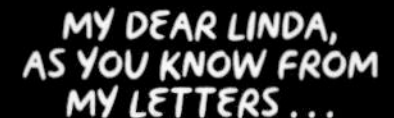

MY DEAR LINDA,
AS YOU KNOW FROM
MY LETTERS . . .

. . . DANNY AND I ARE
LEAVING THE PARK.

I HOPE YOU
UNDERSTAND.

L. LEER

I KNOW THESE MOUNTAINS WERE ONCE ALIVE WITH STORIES.

I KNOW BECAUSE I'VE WRITTEN THE BOOKS TO PROVE IT.

BUT WITHOUT YOU, THEY HAVE GONE QUIET.

WHERE I ONCE FOUND INSPIRATION–

THERE IS NOW A SEA OF STONE.

HURRY THIS UP, ELIJAH. WE NEED TO GET BACK!

WHAT DO YOU WANT ME TO DO?!

"...LIVES IN
ETERNITY'S SUNRISE."
—WILLIAM BLAKE

HEY, MS. LEER, JUST WANTED TO SAY—
I MISS WATCHING YOU SKI.

I WAS THINKING OF THE DAY OF YOUR OLYMPIC RUN.
LINDA LEER : USA
13
KRKY

WE ALL GATHERED AT THE BIG HORN TO CHEER YOU ON.

YOU WERE LIKE A COMET.
NO ONE COULD TURN AWAY.

WHEN YOU MOVED BACK HOME, THE PARK WAS REJUVENATED.
OUR BELOVED QUEEN HAD RETURNED TO CLAIM HER KINGDOM.

SIXTY YEARS BEFORE, OSCAR LEER HAD COME HERE IN SEARCH OF A REMEDY FOR HIS FAILING LUNGS.
HE BUILT HIS CASTLE AMID THE COOL, HEALING AIR OF THE ROCKY MOUNTAINS.
BUT HE NEVER FOUND A CURE.

ALONG WITH HIS ESTATE, YOU INHERITED HIS CURSE.
WHEN YOU FELL SICK AND YOUR NIGHTS WERE RESTLESS, WE'D SIT TOGETHER READING POETRY.
BLAKE

I WOULD PRETEND NOT TO NOTICE YOUR WHEEZING BREATH—
OR YOUR BLOOD-SPECKLED HANDKERCHIEF.
...LIVES IN ETERNITY'S SUNRISE.
WILLIAM BLAKE

THEN ONE NIGHT, I CAME TO MEET YOU AND YOU WEREN'T THERE.
THE ROOM WAS ICE-COLD.
I FOLLOWED YOUR FOOTPRINTS TO THE MAZE.
THEY WAVERED, LIKE DANCE STEPS.
I WAS LED THROUGH THE WINDING PATHS . . .
. . . UNTIL I FOUND YOU LYING IN THE FRESH SNOW.
THE MOONLIGHT WAS BLUE ON YOUR BARE SKIN.
YOU WERE ASLEEP AT LAST, PEACEFUL AND DREAMING.

YOU CAN CALL ME SUPERSTITIOUS, BUT I BELIEVE, WHEN SOMEONE'S GONE–
YOU CAN FIND THEM IN THE THINGS THEY LOVED.
BLAKE

BLAKE

BLAKE

LOS ANGELES. A PARTY HOSTED BY GLOBAL STUDIOS!

I...
I REMEMBER THIS NIGHT.
I WAS THERE TO TALK ABOUT ADAPTING MY LATEST BOOK.
THE STUDIO WAS COURTING LINDA, TOO. THEY WANTED TO MAKE A FILM ABOUT HER.

THIS IS THE DAY YOUR MOTHER AND I MET, DANNY. THE OLYMPIC ATHLETE AND THE HORROR WRITER.
WHAT A PAIR WE WERE!

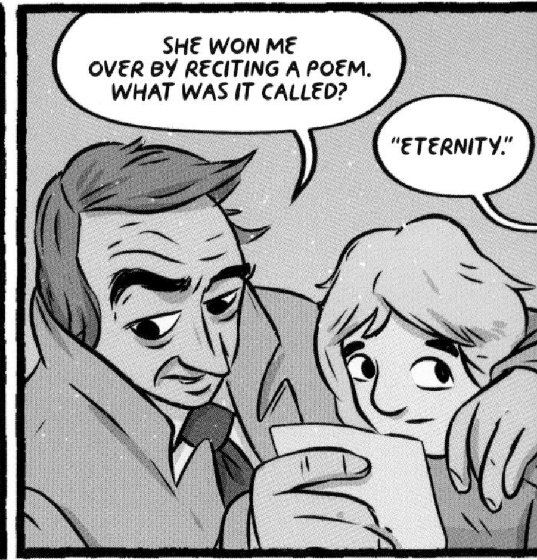
SHE WON ME OVER BY RECITING A POEM. WHAT WAS IT CALLED?
"ETERNITY."

"HE WHO BINDS TO HIMSELF A JOY DOES THE WINGED LIFE DESTROY—
HE WHO KISSES THE JOY AS IT FLIES LIVES IN ETERNITY'S SUNRISE."
THE GREAT RED DRAGON AND THE WOMAN CLOTHED WITH THE SUN, 1805
YOU KNOW, THEY WOULD SAY WILLIAM BLAKE HAD AN IMAGINATION SO POWERFUL HE COULD SEE ANGELS.
AND WHERE THERE ARE ANGELS . . .
NO MATTER HOW DARK IT GOT, LINDA COULD SEE THE LIGHT FIGHTING TO BREAK THROUGH.
THAT'S WHY YOU LOVE HER, JACK.
THAT'S WHY WE ALL LOVE HER.

THAT WAS BRAVE, RENA. YOU WERE SO—
HONEST.
JACK AND MY DAD WERE BEST FRIENDS. I'VE KNOWN HIM SINCE I WAS DANNY'S AGE.

HE'S ALWAYS HAD A DARK CLOUD HANGING OVER HIM. I'M NOT SURE HE'LL EVER GET OUT FROM UNDER IT.

COME ON, LET'S GO. WE DON'T WANT TO MAKE WOODLAND WAIT FOR US.

HEY—
YOU COULDA SAID SOMETHING BACK THERE. YOU'RE A PART OF THE STORY, TOO, YOU KNOW.
IF WE DON'T GET BACK AND SAVE THE HOTEL, THERE WILL BE NO STORY!

GREAT. WHERE IS THAT KID?

DANNY!

DANNY!
WE'RE LEAVING!

UNLESS YOU'RE MOVING IN?
OK, OK, I'M COMING!

FODOR GLAVA
BORN IN TRANSYLVANIA
DIED DECEMBER 1918

HONK!

WHAT IS THE HOLDUP?!
COME ON, GET OUTTA THE ROAD, YA WEIRDOS!

WHAT THE HECK IS THIS?!

THE STREETS ARE QUICKLY FILLING WITH GHOULS, GHOSTS, AND HORROR FANS, HERE TO CELEBRATE THE LAST NIGHTS OF THE UNDERLOOK HOTEL.
13 KRKY
13 DONNA DUNKIN
EYEWITNESS NEWS

BEEN A LONG WEEK OF WORRYIN' 'BOUT WHAT'S NEXT FOR THE PARK.
TONIGHT WE'RE GONNA JUST ENJOY WHAT WE GOT.

BOO.
MOM?

HELLO, ELIJAH.
AND RENA HALLORANN?! IT'S BEEN A MINUTE!
COOL LOOK, MS. HESS.

LIKE IT? I'M BUFFALO BILL.
WHAT'S LEFT OF HIM, ANYWAY.

EXCUSE ME, ARE YOU SUZY'S MOM?
DANNY?

YOU WON'T REMEMBER ME. I'M EDITH.
IT'LL SOUND STRANGE, BUT I'M YOUR—

I MISSED YOU, KIDDO.

OH.
MY.
GOD.

13
KRKY

IT'S HIM!
COME ON, NED!
FOR CRYIN' OUT—

13
DONNA DUNKIN
EYEWITNESS NEWS

NICE OF YOU TO JOIN US, JACK.

WHAT IS ALL THIS?

CALL IT A FAREWELL PARTY.

WHAT'S WITH THAT CAMERA, KID?

JACK! I WANT YOU TO MEET ANGELA WOODLAND.
SHE'S FROM THE MUSEUM OF FILM.

HELLO, MR. AXWORTH. I'M HERE TO TALK ABOUT PRESERVING YOUR HOTEL AND ITS ARCHIVE—
NO, NO, NO!
I'VE MADE MY DECISION.

IT'S MY *RESPONSIBILITY.* I'M THE CARETAKER.

JACK.

YOU'RE NOT IN THIS ALONE.

WE'RE ALL TRYING TO FIND THE BEST WAY TO MOVE ON.
AND WE THINK YOU SHOULD LISTEN TO WHAT SHE HAS TO SAY.

BIG HORN
DINER

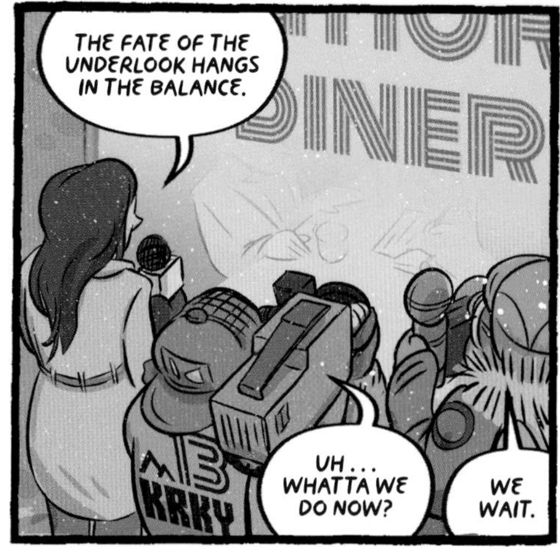
THE FATE OF THE UNDERLOOK HANGS IN THE BALANCE.
UH . . . WHATTA WE DO NOW?
WE WAIT.

HEY, SUZY, WILL THE KIDS AT MY NEW SCHOOL THINK I'M WEIRD?
UNDOUBTEDLY.

MY ADVICE?
KEEP TO YOURSELF. THE LESS THEY KNOW, THE LESS THEY HAVE TO USE AGAINST YOU.
VAMPIRE!

EXACTLY. BELIEVING IN VAMPIRES IS A VERY WEIRD THING TO SAY ALOUD.
NO, LOOK!

IT'S THE VAMPIRE!

WILD WEST TOURS
I TOLD YOU HE WAS REAL!
HOLD ON, DANNY!

EXCUSE ME. ARE YOU—
FODOR GLAVA?!
WHY, YES, I AM.

I KNEW IT! I HAVE A PHOTO OF YOU!

AND YOU'RE—
DANNY AXWORTH.

HOWDY, DANNY!
TALK ABOUT A REAL COLORADO LEGEND!
WHOO DOGGY!
HI!
I'D LIKE YOU TO MEET MY FRIENDS,
COLORADO'S MOST-SPIRITED CHEATER, MURDERER, AND LIAR.

JEFFERSON RANDOLPH SMITH HERE!
BUT YOU CAN CALL ME "SOAPY"!

MY "PRIZE" SOAP RACKET EARNED ME AN' MY GANG A WHOLE LOT OF MONEY.
AND I'D BE AT IT STILL . . .

. . . IF IT WEREN'T FOR THE DARN BULLET LODGED IN MY DARN HEART.

ALFERD PACKER–
BEST TOUR GUIDE IN THE ROCKIES.

SURE, LONG AS YA DON'T RUN OUTTA FOOD.
THEY CALL HIM THE "COLORADO CANNIBAL."

HOLD ON NOW! TECHNICALLY, YA KNOW . . .
. . . IT AIN'T ILLEGAL TO EAT A FELLA.

HELLO!
NAME'S LLOYD OLSEN.
HI, LLOYD! ARE YOU A MURDERER OR SOMETHING?

AW, JUST AN AVERAGE FELLA.
BUT YOU KNOW WHO AIN'T AVERAGE?

MY BEST FRIEND–
MIRACLE MIKE!

WELL, FOLKS USUALLY PAY TO HEAR THE STORY OF FODOR GLAVA . . .

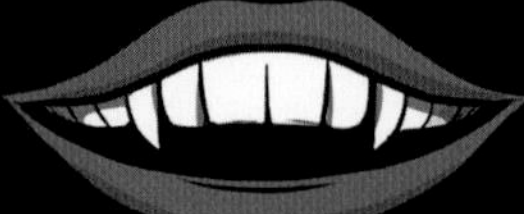

. . . BUT IT'S A SPECIAL DAY. Y'ALL CAN HAVE IT FOR FREE.

"I WORKED MY WAY UP THE RANKS FROM MINER TO UNDERLOOKER, SUPERVISING THE NIGHT-SHIFT OPERATION OF THE MINE'S DEEPEST TUNNELS.

HOTEL
"I'D BE SEEN WALKING HOME ALONE, COVERED IN SOOT, MELDING WITH THE LONG DARKNESS THAT COMES RIGHT BEFORE THE DAWN.

"TO THE TOWNSFOLK, I REMAINED A STRANGER FROM A DISTANT LAND, AND I DIED IN 1918 WITHOUT FRIENDS OR FAMILY TO MOURN ME.
FODOR GLA
"BUT THAT WAS NOT MY END, NOT BY A LONG SHOT.

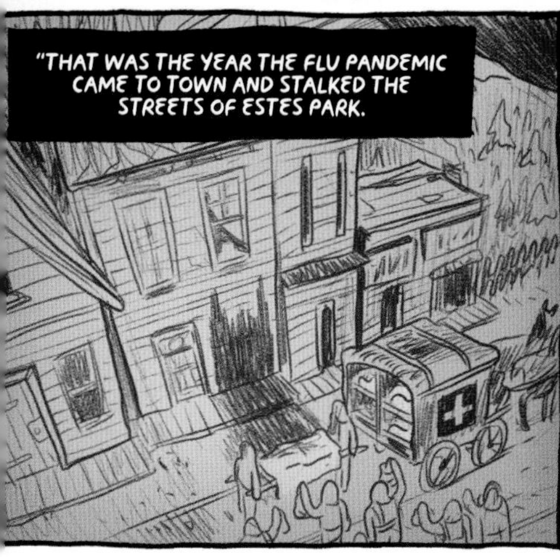
"THAT WAS THE YEAR THE FLU PANDEMIC CAME TO TOWN AND STALKED THE STREETS OF ESTES PARK.

"AND TO THE FEARFUL AND SUPERSTITIOUS, DEATH LOOKED SUSPICIOUSLY LIKE ME.

"TO RID THEIR TOWN OF MY CURSED SHADOW, THEY CAME TO DIG ME UP.
"RUMOR HAD IT MY TEETH WERE OVERSIZE AND BLOODSTAINED, MY FINGERNAILS LONG AND POINTED.

"WITHOUT FURTHER REASON, A STAKE WAS DRIVEN INTO MY HEART.
"SOMEONE HAD JUST READ DRACULA, APPARENTLY.

"DECADES PASSED.

"THE MINE CLOSED.

"BUT THE TALE OF MY SECOND DEATH LINGERED.

"VISITORS CLAIMED THAT AN OAK TREE GREW FROM THE MURDEROUS STAKE—
"AND A WILD ROSEBUSH GREW FROM MY VILLAINOUS FINGERNAILS.
"IT WASN'T LONG UNTIL I WAS REVIVED AGAIN . . .

"...NOT AS FODOR GLAVA, BUT AS A SOULLESS DEVIL.
"I BECAME A BESTSELLER.
"I BECAME A BLOCKBUSTER."

NOW I LIVE FOREVER IN OTHER PEOPLE'S WORLDS AND STORIES—
WITHOUT EVEN A SENSE OF SELF TO KEEP ME COMPANY.

IF THAT ISN'T A CURSE, I DON'T KNOW WHAT IS.

HEARD HIM TELL THAT STORY A COUPLE THOUSAND TIMES.
MIKE AND I STILL GET CHOKED UP.

I'M SORRY MY DAD BROUGHT YOU BACK TO LIFE, MR. GLAVA.

REST EASY, FRIEND.
I ONLY PLAY A VAMPIRE TO PAY THE BILLS.

WILD WEST TOURS
20% OFF

OH, THANK YOU! I'M LEAVING SOON, BUT SUZY CAN USE IT!
GEE, THANKS.

I DON'T THINK YOUR FRIEND CARES FOR LOCAL HISTORY.
ACTUALLY, SHE CARES A LOT!
I DON'T WANT TO LIVE IN THE PAST, IF THAT'S WHAT YOU MEAN.

HISTORY IS NEVER FAR BEHIND US, MS. HESS.
SOMETIMES WE EVEN FIND OUR-SELVES STANDING IN ITS MIDST.
BIG HORN

BIG HORN
DINER

BIG HORN
DINER

I...
I'VE BEEN READING MY BOOKS THIS PAST WEEK.
BIG HORN
KRKT

IT SEEMS I'VE NEVER BEEN VERY GOOD WITH ENDINGS.
NONETHELESS, WE HAVE REACHED THE END OF OUR STORY TOGETHER, AND I'D LIKE TO SAY—
YEAH, YOUR ENDINGS STINK!
YOU TEARING DOWN OUR HOTEL OR WHAT?!
YEAH! JUST TELL US!

WELL, MS. WOODLAND CAN SPEAK TO THAT.
I'LL KEEP IT BRIEF.

THE UNDERLOOK HOTEL, IT SEEMS, IS AN INVALUABLE ARTIFACT OF CINEMA.
AND MR. AXWORTH, IN ALL HIS GENEROSITY, HAS DONATED HIS HOTEL TO MY MUSEUM.
REST ASSURED, WE ARE COMMITTED TO PRESERVING ITS UNIQUE LEGACY.
THANK YOU.

CINEMA?
SHE MEAN MOVIES?
SUZY!
WHAT'S SHE MEAN BY "PRESERVE"?
LIKE SEAL IT IN A JELLY JAR?
HM, THAT IS AN EXCELLENT QUESTION.

MS. WOODLAND, WHAT DO YOU MEAN "PRESERVE" THE HOTEL?
THE UNDERLOOK WILL BE REGISTERED AS A HISTORICAL LANDMARK AND DEACTIVATED AS SOON AS POSSIBLE.
EXCUSE ME, "DEACTIVATED"?

WHILE IT IS STILL MAJESTIC FROM AFAR, BUILDING RECORDS SHOW THE UNDERLOOK IS RAPIDLY DETERIORATING.
COME ON, IT JUST NEEDS A NEW BOILER!
AREN'T YOU GONNA FIX IT UP?

AS I SAID, THE MUSEUM IS COMMITTED TO THE PRESERVATION OF THIS VERY SPECIAL BUILDING—
BUT WE ARE NOT IN THE HOTEL-MANAGEMENT BUSINESS.

SHE ISN'T SAVING THE HOTEL; SHE'S TURNING IT INTO TAXIDERMY. WE HAVE TO STOP HER!
IT'S BETTER THAN BEING DEMOLISHED.

RIGHT?

WHOA, WHOA.
WHAT'S WITH THE LOOK?

LET ME GO.

LIKE YOU SAID— WE'RE AT OUR BEST AT THE BITTER END.
THIS ISN'T THE BITTER END, ELIJAH. WE DIDN'T LOSE.

TELL THAT TO HER.

UH, HI, I'M RENA.

EGGS
COFFEE
2.49
I USED TO PLAY FOR THE PARK.
STOMP 'EM, YETIS!
HA HA, YEAH.
MY GREAT-GREAT-GRANDPA HELPED BUILD LEER'S BIG, FANCY HOTEL.
HALF A CENTURY LATER, MY DAD WAS RUNNING THE KITCHEN.
THERE ARE A MILLION STORIES LIVING IN THAT OLD PLACE.
I KNOW MINE'S ONE OF THEM.
I'LL TELL YA, I'M SCARED THEY'RE ALL ABOUT TO DISAPPEAR—
AND NO DOUBT SOME OF THEM WILL.
BUT I DON'T THINK TODAY SHOULD BE ABOUT SAYING GOODBYE.

SEEING AS HOW WE'RE ALL TOGETHER—
I SAY WE START SOMETHING NEW!
LIKE WHAT?

LIKE A—

A—

1876 - 1976
76
CENTENNIAL
LIKE A CELEBRATION!

A SPECIAL DAY, NOT JUST FOR HISTORY—
A DAY FOR MAKING NEW STORIES!

A DAY DEDICATED TO
ALL THE PEOPLE WHO FIND
THEMSELVES OUT HERE IN THE
MIDDLE OF NOWHERE!

RADIO CLUBS

COME OOOOON!
WE'RE MISSING THE
COFFIN RACE FINALS!

THIS IS THE
LAST OF MY FILM,
ELIJAH.

I'LL MAKE
IT COUNT!

YOU KNOW, THE LAST TIME YOU STOOD AT MY COUNTER–
I WAS SELLING YOU TYPEWRITER RIBBONS.
AKLER BRAND.
YOU WOULD ORDER THEM SPECIAL FOR ME.

SALE
HOW CAN YOU REMEMBER THAT DETAIL AND NOT WHAT'S BEHIND YOUR BEDROOM DOOR?

GEESH, SUZY.
NO, THAT'S A FAIR QUESTION.

MY TYPEWRITER GAVE ME A VOICE. IT GAVE ME FRIENDS. IT GAVE ME FAMILY.
SOME THINGS ARE SO INSTRUMENTAL TO WHO YOU ARE THEY CANNOT BE FORGOTTEN.
OK, THEN WHY THROW IT AWAY?
HOW DO YOU KNOW I THREW IT AWAY?
GEESH, SUZY.
HA HA, OOPS.

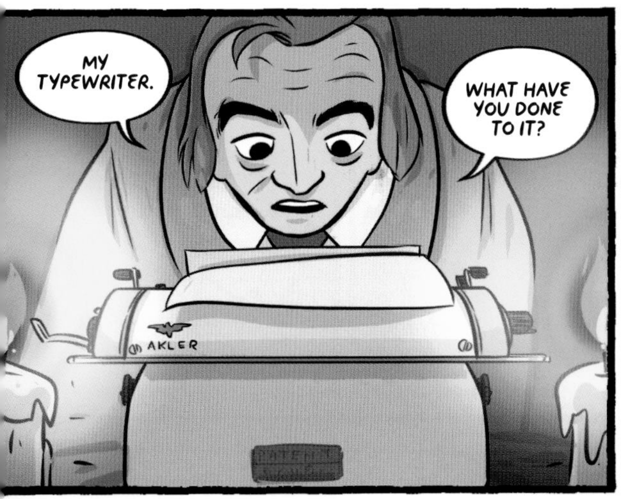
MY TYPEWRITER.
WHAT HAVE YOU DONE TO IT?
AKLER

I JAZZED IT UP. YOU KNOW, FOR THE...
...TOURISTS.

YES, YES, BUT WHAT DOES IT DO?

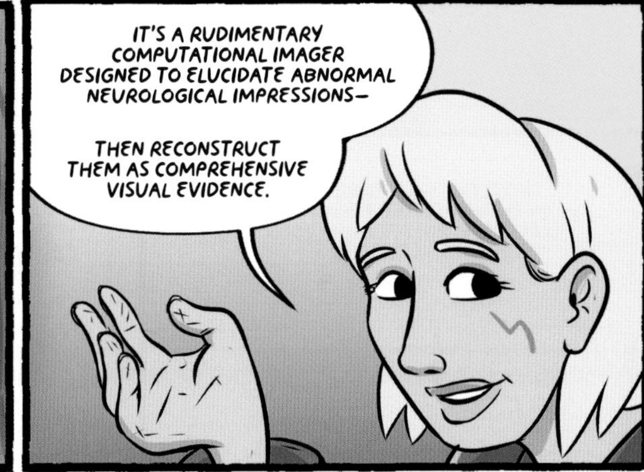
IT'S A RUDIMENTARY COMPUTATIONAL IMAGER DESIGNED TO ELUCIDATE ABNORMAL NEUROLOGICAL IMPRESSIONS—
THEN RECONSTRUCT THEM AS COMPREHENSIVE VISUAL EVIDENCE.

I CALL IT THE
GHOST WRITER.
AKLER

DING!
AKLER

WHAT DO YOU SAY, MR. AXWORTH?
WANT TO KNOW WHAT THE CREEPY VOICES IN YOUR HEAD HAVE TO SAY?

HM, WELL, I AM THE KING OF HORROR.

THAT'S THE SPIRIT.

DON'T BE SCARED. I'LL EXPLAIN HOW IT WORKS.

FIRST, THE NEURAL PICKUPS IN THE HEADBAND TRANSMIT ELECTRICAL PULSES FROM YOUR BRAIN'S NERVE CELLS.
TABLE SURFACE
THEN THE SIGNALS PASS THROUGH A HEAT-SENSITIVE METAL FILAMENT, ERODING HOLES IN A PHOTOSENSITIVE CYLINDER.

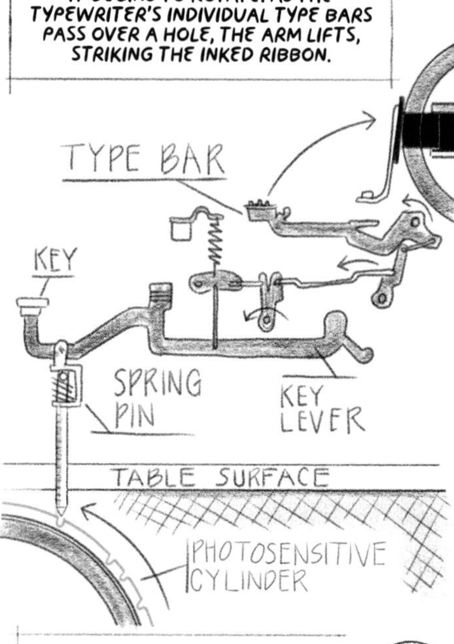
WHEN THE CYLINDER IS FULL, IT BEGINS TO ROTATE. AS THE TYPEWRITER'S INDIVIDUAL TYPE BARS PASS OVER A HOLE, THE ARM LIFTS, STRIKING THE INKED RIBBON.
TYPE BAR
KEY
SPRING PIN
KEY LEVER
TABLE SURFACE
PHOTOSENSITIVE CYLINDER
FINALLY, AN EMBOSSED LETTER LEAVES AN IMPRINT ON THE PAPER, AND THE MESSAGE BEGINS TO APPEAR.
X

CLEVER, THOUGH NOT VERY SUPERNATURAL.
THAT'S WHERE MOM'S CUSTOM AMPLIFIER COMES INTO PLAY.

COME ON, YOU'RE RUINING THE ILLUSION!

IT FILTERS OUT ERRANT SIGNALS.
ERRANT SIGNALS?

IT'S HER SPOOKY TERM FOR "UNIDENTIFIABLE STRAY NOISE."
YOU REALLY ARE NO FUN, SUZY.

HOLD ON, JACK. I'M GOING TO TRY TO TUNE IN TO A BESTSELLER.

IT'S A JOKE! SEE, I CAN BE FUN!

YOU DON'T THINK MUCH OF ME, DO YOU?
ACTUALLY—
I'VE THOUGHT ABOUT YOU A LOT.

I JUST DON'T UNDERSTAND YOU.

MECHANICAL SYSTEMS, COMPUTATIONAL STUFF— IT CLICKS FOR ME.

BUT THE WAY YOUR STORIES WORK . . . IT'S TOO ABSTRACT. YOUR BOOKS ARE LIKE READING A MATHEMATICAL PROOF.
YOU KNOW WHAT I MEAN?
NO, I DO NOT.

A PROOF STARTS WITH A CONCLUSION, SOMETHING THE MATHEMATICIAN BELIEVES TO BE TRUE.

HALCYON TRIANGLE
LET'S SAY . . .
. . . A PARTICULAR GEOMETRIC SHAPE.
RED MOUNTAIN
UNDERLOOK
MT. OLYMPUS
GLACIER CREEK

THE MATHEMATICIAN STARTS SEARCHING TILL THEY FIND THE RIGHT CONDITIONS TO AFFIRM THEIR CONCLUSION.
IF IT HAS VERTICES LIKE A TRIANGLE–
AND A CENTER LIKE A TRIANGLE–
IT MUST BE A TRIANGLE, RIGHT?!
BUT THE THING IS, WHEN YOU ENGINEER SOMETHING IN REVERSE . . .
. . . ALL YOU GET IS AN ILLUSION.
UNDERLOOK
GLACIER CREEK
I'M NOT TRYING TO HURT YOUR FEELINGS.
I JUST DON'T UNDERSTAND WHY YOU BELIEVE YOUR BOOKS ARE SO FREAKING IMPORTANT . . .
. . . WHEN THE STORIES IN THEM AREN'T REAL.

I'M SORRY, JACK. MY DAUGHTER GETS A THRILL OUT OF RATIONALIZING EVERYTHING.
I DO NOT!
DO I LOOK THRILLED?
I'M SORRY, I CAN'T EXPLAIN THE PHENOMENON OF MY WORK, OTHER THAN TO SAY . . .
. . . LIFE IS A LONELY JOURNEY, SUZY.
WE WALK ALONE, WITH ONLY SHADOWS TO KEEP US COMPANY.
BOOKS ARE BEACONS.
THEY HELP US FIND ONE ANOTHER.
YOU BELIEVE THAT?
I DO.
THEN YOU MUST REALLY MISS BEING A WRITER.
NOT AS MUCH AS I MISS THE PEOPLE I MET ALONG THE WAY.

I SHOULD SAY...
...I THINK YOU'RE BRAVE FOR GIVING UP YOUR HOTEL.

I KNOW IT'S NOT WHAT YOU WANTED.
NO.

BUT IT IS WHAT LINDA WOULD HAVE WANTED.
HOW DO YOU KNOW THAT?

CALL IT AN ERRANT SIGNAL.

DING!

COME ON OUTSIDE, Y'ALL!
THEY'RE SHOOTING OFF FIREWORKS!

DANNY, YOU FORGOT YOUR GLOVES.
DANNY'S WITH ELIJAH.

UH, NO, HE'S NOT.

ARE YOU KIDDING ME?
YOU REALIZE IT'S AFTER MIDNIGHT!

IT'S FINE, MS. H. HE MUST HAVE GOTTEN CAUGHT UP—
RENA?

WHERE IS MY SON?

I...
I DON'T KNOW.

DON'T WORRY, JACK.
I'M SURE HE'S RIGHT OUTSIDE.

SALE
click clack click clack click clack click clack click

click clack click clack

click clack
click clack
click clack
click clack
click clack

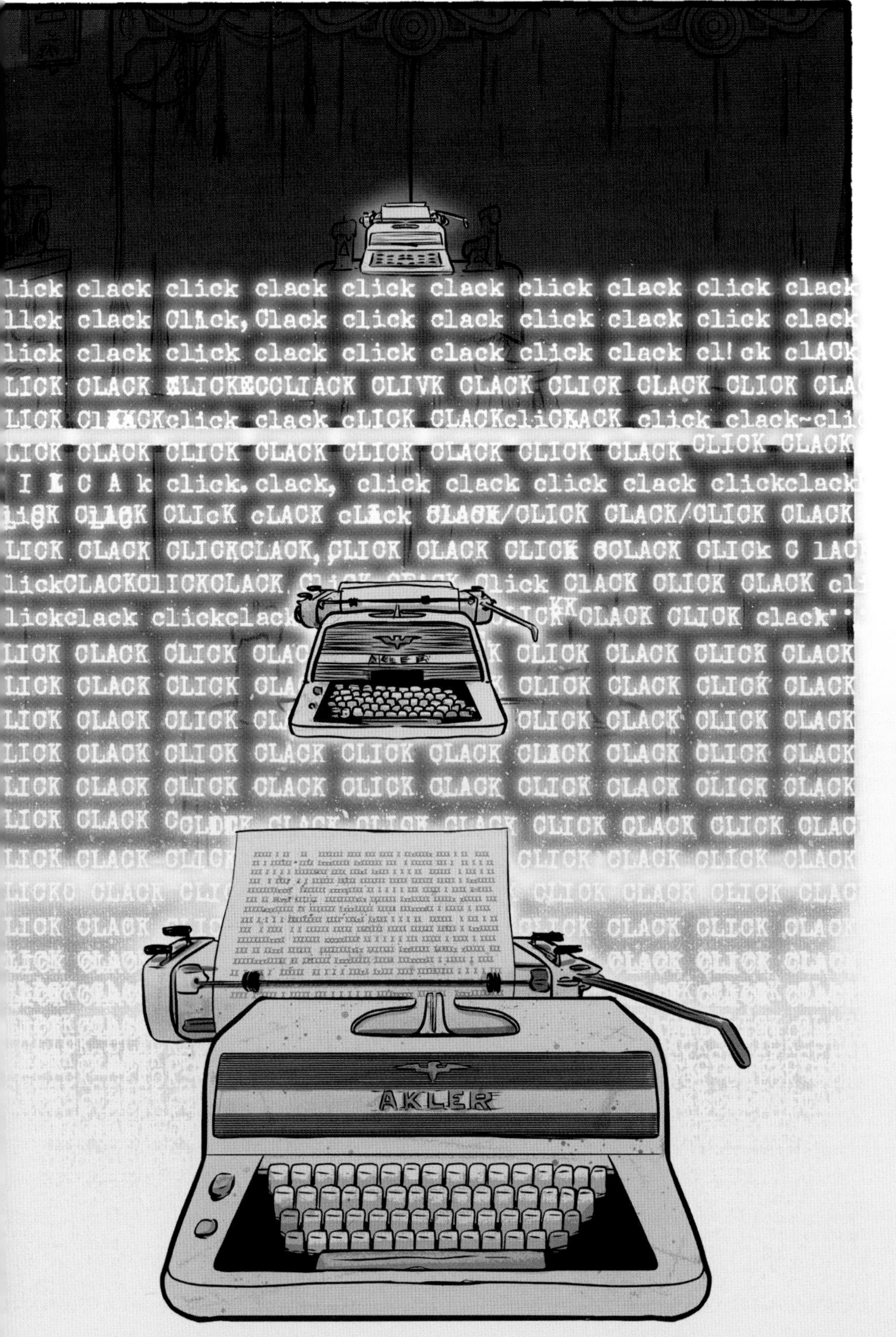
lick clack click clack click clack click clack click clack
llck clack Click, Clack click clack click clack click clack
lick clack click clack click clack click clack cl!ck clACK
LICK CLACK CLICK CLACK CLICK CLACK CLICK CLACK
LICK CLACK CLICK CLACK CLICK CLACK CLICK CLACK CLICK CLACK
LICK CLACK CLICK CLACK CLICK CLACK CLICK CLACK CLICK CLACK
AKLER
AKLER

ESTES PARK, COLORADO

HAVE YOU SEEN A LITTLE BOY?
TEN YEARS OLD.
BLOND HAIR.

IT'S GETTING AWFULLY COLD OUT.

DON'T WORRY, MR. A.
WE'LL FIND YOUR SON.

ESTES PARK
THE FUNICULAR IS GONE!
DANNY MUST HAVE TAKEN IT BACK TO THE HOTEL.

WHY WOULD HE GO ALONE?
HE ISN'T ALONE.

WHAT ARE WE WAITING FOR? BRING THE CAR DOWN, SUZY!
I CAN'T! THE CONTROLS ARE LOCKED. IT'S STUCK AT THE TOP.

HOP IN MY TRUCK. WE'LL TAKE THE OLD HOTEL SERVICE ROAD.

IT HASN'T BEEN PLOWED SINCE MONDAY!
A RANGER IS ALWAYS PREPARED!

HEY, CHUCK! UNLOCK THE BACK!
YOU KIDDING ME, SUZ? THIS ISN'T A JOY RIDE.

MOM!
TRUST US, HON. WE'RE ON IT.

WE HAVE TO FOLLOW THEM.
WHERE'S ELIJAH? WE NEED HIS CRABBY TAXI GUY.
ELIJAH!
DID YOU SEE THOSE TIRES? NO TAXI IS GETTING UP THAT ROAD.

UNLESS YOU HAVE THREE PAIRS OF SNOWSHOES, WE'RE STUCK.
HEY, YOU GUYS!

OH GREAT, IT'S DUNKIN.
SHE SAW DANNY! TELL THEM!

AFTER THE COFFIN RACE, I SAW YOUR FRIEND TALKING TO A VAMPIRE.
CARE TO NARROW IT DOWN? THIS TOWN IS CRAWLING WITH VAMPIRES!

HE HAD A ROSE ON HIS COAT, DIDN'T HE?
YOU KNOW HIM?

DANNY AND I MET HIM YESTERDAY. VERY CHARMING GUY—
EVEN FOR A VAMPIRE.
HOLY SMOKE, DANNY'S BEEN KIDNAPPED?!

HEY, DUNKIN. YOU'VE GOT FOUR-WHEEL DRIVE ON THAT VAN, DON'T YOU?

FORGET IT.
I DON'T GO ANYWHERE WITHOUT A CAMERAMAN.

SMILE!

13

MOVE OVER, DUNKIN.
NO ONE KNOWS THAT ROAD LIKE I DO.
A MOBILE EDITING BAY!
SOOOO COOL!

HEY! DON'T YOU TOUCH THAT!
click! click!

BUCKLE UP BACK THERE!
IT'S ABOUT TO GET BUMPY.
OK!
SOMEONE EXPLAIN THE DEAL WITH THIS VAMPIRE!
WHAT'S HE WANT WITH DANNY?
HIS REAL NAME IS WARD BARLOW.
I INTERVIEWED HIM ON MONDAY. HE'S A PARK-HISTORY BUFF. HE KNEW A LOT ABOUT THE HOTEL, BUT HE DIDN'T STRIKE ME AS A BIG 'LURKER.
REINDEER!
HOTEL
EST. 1909

CAN I SEE THE FOOTAGE FROM YOUR INTERVIEW?
BARLOW INTERVIEW PROPERTY OF KRKY-13
HOW DARE YOU TRY TO SCOOP MY STORY!
WHERE'S YOUR JOURNALISTIC INTEGRITY?

I'M NOT SCOOPING!
I'M LOOKING FOR CLUES!
CLUES?!
THIS IS A NEWS VAN! IT'S NOT THE MYSTERY MACHINE!

STOP!

SKREECH

OOF!
CAN YOU STOP DOING THAT?!

MOM!
ARE YOU OK?

I'M FINE.
WE'RE ALL FINE.
JUST STUCK!

HOW ARE YOU HERE?!
YOU'D BETTER NOT BE DRIVING!

I'M NOT! LISTEN, DANNY'S WITH A VAMPIRE! WE HAVE TO KEEP GOING!
NO WAY! YOU WAIT RIGHT THERE!

IT'S OK, MS. HESS. I'VE GOT THAT WALKIE FROM YOUR SHOP!

SUZY MARIE HESS!
WHAT DID I SAY?!

YOU TOLD ME TO WATCH OUT FOR MY FRIENDS.

I DID, DIDN'T I?

HERE WE GO.
HOLD ON.
WE'RE NOT GOING ANYWHERE UNTIL WE CAN TRUST EACH OTHER.

FINE.
I'LL LET YOU SEE MY FOOTAGE...
BARLOW INTERVIEW

...IF YOU LET ME INTO THE UNDERLOOK.
DEAL.

AND I WANT AN EXCLUSIVE INTERVIEW WITH JACK AXWORTH—
VROOM
DON'T PUSH IT.

BE CAREFUL WITH THAT! IT'S A $100,000 SYSTEM!
RELAX, DUNKIN. ELIJAH KNOWS HIS STUFF.
Scenic Bywa

HE'S THE VIDEOGRAPHER FOR HIS SCHOOL'S ATHLETIC DEPARTMENT.

AWW!
YOU REMEMBERED!

ZODAK
Z 120
EDWARD BARLOW
INTERVIEW

THERE'S A CERTAIN BEAUTY TO THESE MOUNTAINS.
IT DRAWS PEOPLE TO THEM.
SOMETIMES PEOPLE MISTAKE THAT BEAUTY FOR GENEROSITY.

"TAKE THOSE MINERS WHO FOUNDED OUR TOWN. CLEVER FOLKS— INVENTORS, ENGINEERS—
"BUT NOT TOO BRIGHT.
"SPENT A FORTUNE LOOKIN' FOR A FORTUNE."

THAT'S WHEN THE OUT-OF-TOWNER LEER SWOOPED IN LIKE A VULTURE—
WHAT'S HE TALKING ABOUT?

WHEN THE MINERS WENT BROKE, THEY SOLD OSCAR LEER THE LAND.
IT'S TRUE. I'VE SEEN THE DEED.

WARD TOLD DANNY THAT THE VAMPIRE WORKED IN THE MINE. HE CALLED HIMSELF . . .
. . . THE ORIGINAL UNDERLURKER.

HE SAID ESTES PARK CURSED HIM—
AND NOW HE CAN NEVER DIE.

AREN'T YOU TWO CUTE.

DEDUCTIVE REASONING IS NOT CUTE!
CREEPING EACH OTHER OUT WITH AN OLD-TIME FOLKTALE? IT'S CUTE.
HEY, WHAT FOLKTALE?

"THE GIRL IN THE CAVE"—
OF COURSE.

WHAT?!

OK, YOU TWO ARE CUTE, BUT THIS IS ADORABLE.
GIRL IN THE CAVE

BUT WHERE DOES THIS STORY COME FROM?!
YOU DON'T KNOW?
IT'S A CAUTIONARY TALE. BEEN AROUND FOREVER.

PARENTS USE IT TO SCARE KIDS FROM WANDERING INTO ABANDONED MINESHAFTS.
GIRL IN THE

OF COURSE! THE CAVE IS A MINE! HOW DID I NOT FIGURE THAT OUT?!
DON'T WORRY, SHERLOCK. WE WON'T TELL ANYONE.

HUH. YOU GAVE THE GIRL A HAPPY ENDING.
WHAT'S WRONG WITH A HAPPY ENDING?

WELL, IT RUINS THE LESSON.

THE KID HAS TO DIE—
OR THE STORY IS POINTLESS.

OK, THAT'S ENOUGH STORY TIME.

LET'S HUNT A VAMPIRE.

OH, MR. VAMPIRE...

WHERE ARE YOU?!

WARD COAXED DANNY INTO BRINGING HIM HERE. I TOLD YOU HE WAS CHARMING!

AND A CON ARTIST! AFTER THE INTERVIEW, HE TRIED TO SELL ME "EXCLUSIVE" PHOTOS FROM INSIDE THE HOTEL.
FAKES. HE'D HAVE TO HAVE–

TAKEN THEM RIGHT OFF THE HOTEL WALL.

IMPOSSIBLE! I KEEP THIS PLACE LOCKED TIGHT!
UM . . .
HE MIGHT HAVE FOUND A WAY IN.

WHY DIDN'T YOU TELL ME YOU LOST YOUR KEY?!
EXCUSE ME?
I HAVE A REPUTATION FOR BEING RESPONSIBLE!

HEY, ELIJAH KNEW ABOUT THE KEY, TOO!
FINE. BLAME ME!
LET'S JUST FIND THIS CREEP!

HE'S RIGHT. SO WHERE DO WE START?
SPLIT UP AND SEARCH ALL THE ROOMS?
EASIER SAID THAN DONE. WE NEED TO KNOW WHAT THE VAMPIRE IS LOOKING FOR.

WELL, WE KNOW HE HAS DANNY'S KEY, SO HE'S PROBABLY AFTER THE FILM COLLECTION.
STEALING THE FILMS IS POINTLESS NOW.
HE MUST BE AFTER SOMETHING WE DON'T KNOW ABOUT.
WHO KNOWS MORE ABOUT THE HOTEL THAN WE DO?

NO ONE. WELL, THAT RUBRIK GUY SURE THINKS HE DOES . . .
DR. RUBRIK!

THE VAMPIRE SOLD THE PHOTOS TO RUBRIK! I REMEMBER RENA SPOTTED THEM ON HIS WALL.

BUT PHOTOS WEREN'T ENOUGH TO PROVE HIS THEORY. HE NEEDED DANNY'S KEY.

RIGHT BEFORE WE LEFT, RUBRIK SAID TO US–

"DON'T YOU SEE? THE SECRET LIES WITH LINDA LEER!"

HER KEY UNLOCKS MORE THAN A ROOM OF OLD MOVIES–
AND THE VAMPIRE KNOWS IT.

ZOINKS!
ALL WE NEED IS A TALKING GREAT DANE TO SOLVE THE MYSTERY, RIGHT, GANG?!

YOU HAVE ALL THE LEER FAMILY RECORDS, RIGHT?
YEAH, THEY'RE IN MY OFFICE.

OH, WHAT, Y'ALL ARE TOO COOL FOR CARTOONS?

THAT'S A LOT OF RECORDS.
WHAT CAN I SAY? THIS PLACE IS OLD.
LEER
THUNK

REMEMBER, A HAUNTOLOGIST WOULD BE LOOKING FOR ONE THING—
PIECES OF THE PAST, DISRUPTING THE PRESENT.

WELL, WHEN I'M RESEARCHING A STORY,
I START BY LOOKING FOR ANYTHING OUT OF THE ORDINARY.

LIKE A REALLY OLD UNOPENED LETTER?
GOD. AREN'T YOU SICK OF MAIL?

WHY WOULD THE HALCYON MINING COMPANY SEND A LETTER TO . . .
. . . ITSELF?
LET ME SEE THAT.
HALCYON WONDERVIEW AVE. ESTES PARK, CO
HALCYON WONDERVIEW AVE. ESTES PARK, CO

WHAT YOU HAVE HERE IS A PATENT-APPLICATION LETTER.

WHEN APPLYING FOR A PATENT, YOU MAIL YOURSELF A COPY OF THE SCHEMATIC AS A BACKUP RECORD.
SCHEMATIC?
LET ME SEE THAT.

IT'S SOME KIND OF MINING HOIST . . .

. . . AND I'VE SEEN IT BEFORE.

SUZY, WHAT THE HECK?!
LOOK!
THEY REALLY BUILT IT!

1906 - HALCYON MINERS, ROMERO, GLAVA, OLSEN

AND THIS GUY? THIS IS FODOR GLAVA. HE WORKED FOR THE MINE. HIS JOB TITLE WAS UNDERLOOKER.
WHY'S HE BLURRY?
tap tap tap

SOME OLD CAMERAS HAVE MIRRORS!
VAMPIRES DON'T SHOW UP IN MIRRORS!

SO YOU THINK THE VAMPIRE CAME BACK TO THE HOTEL . . .
. . . BECAUSE HE WANTS HIS OLD JOB BACK?

AN UNDERLOOKER'S JOB WAS TO MANAGE THE MINE.
HE WOULD KNOW EVERYTHING THAT'S DOWN THERE.

SO . . . WHAT'S DOWN THERE?

THE GIRL IN THE CAVE . . .
THE EVIL SPIRIT GUARDS A TREASURE.

THAT'S A STORY. IT ISN'T REAL.
RIGHT.
BUT WHAT IF WARD BARLOW THINKS IT IS?

WE FIND THIS TREASURE, WE FIND DANNY.

I HAVE TO SAY, I'VE DONE MY RESEARCH ON THIS HOTEL–
AND I'VE NEVER COME ACROSS ANY MINING HOIST.
THE ENGINEERS MUST HAVE ABANDONED THIS PATENT WHEN THEY SOLD THE LAND TO OSCAR LEER.
NO PATENT.
NO RECORD.
PATENT APPLIC
CONTROL KEY
FIG 1
FIG 2
FIG 3
CLAMP MOUNT
RUBRIK BELIEVED IN IT–
EVEN IF HE COULDN'T SEE IT.
IF THIS THING WAS BUILT IN THE MIDDLE OF THE HOTEL, WE'D NOTICE, RIGHT?
NO, WE WOULDN'T.
BECAUSE IT DOESN'T LOOK LIKE A HOIST–
IT LOOKS LIKE AN ELEVATOR.

PATENT APPLICATION
CONTROL KEY
FIG 1
FIG 2
FIG 3
CLAMP MOUNT
FIG 4
FIG 4
HALCYON MINE WINDER

NOW THAT'S BONKERS!
IS THAT LINDA LEER'S KEY?

"THE CONTROL KEY ENGAGES A CLAMP THAT MOUNTS THE LIFT CAGE TO A CORKSCREW RAIL."
I DON'T BELIEVE IT.

IT'S TRUE. WE ALL FELT IT WORKING.

THE FREAKING ELEVATOR ROTATES?!
THE FREAKING ELEVATOR ROTATES.
GUESS THAT EXPLAINS THE SECRET MOVIE ROOM.
KINDA RUINS THE MAGIC, HONESTLY.
THAT'S ENGINEERING FOR YOU.
LEER
LEER

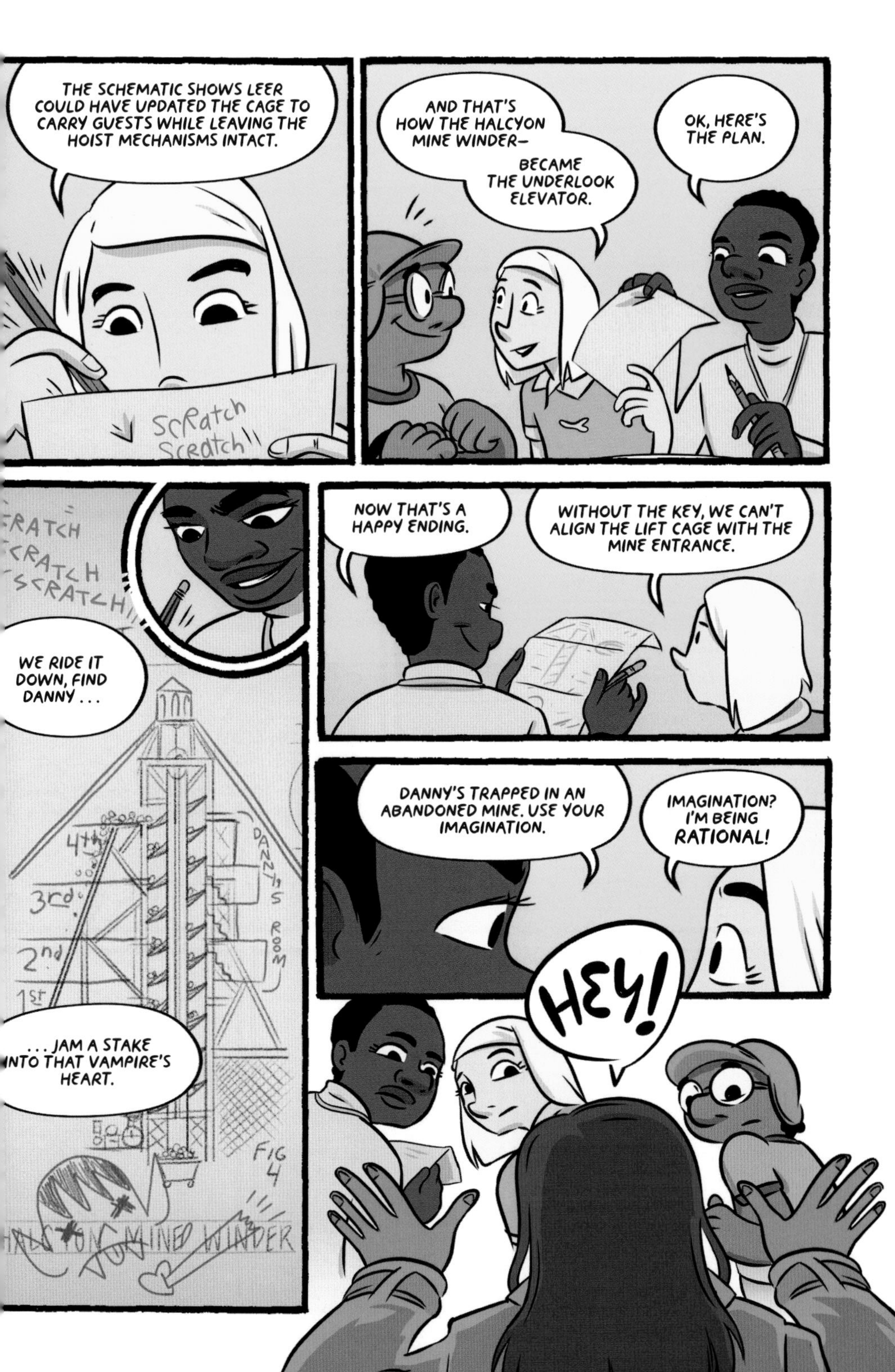
THE SCHEMATIC SHOWS LEER COULD HAVE UPDATED THE CAGE TO CARRY GUESTS WHILE LEAVING THE HOIST MECHANISMS INTACT.
SCRATCH
SCRATCH
AND THAT'S HOW THE HALCYON MINE WINDER—
BECAME THE UNDERLOOK ELEVATOR.
OK, HERE'S THE PLAN.
SCRATCH
SCRATCH
SCRATCH
WE RIDE IT DOWN, FIND DANNY . . .
4th
3rd
2nd
1st
DANNY'S ROOM
FIG 4
HALCYON MINE WINDER
. . . JAM A STAKE INTO THAT VAMPIRE'S HEART.
NOW THAT'S A HAPPY ENDING.
WITHOUT THE KEY, WE CAN'T ALIGN THE LIFT CAGE WITH THE MINE ENTRANCE.
DANNY'S TRAPPED IN AN ABANDONED MINE. USE YOUR IMAGINATION.
IMAGINATION? I'M BEING RATIONAL!
HEY!

I'VE HEARD ENOUGH ABOUT VAMPIRES, CURSES, AND MIND WINDERS!
MINE WINDERS.

WHATEVER!
NO WAY ARE YOU KIDS GOING INTO AN ABANDONED MINE!

ZOINKS, MS. DUNKIN!
WE'D NEVER DO THAT.
JINKIES, US KIDS GET SCARED!
WE JUST LIKE SOLVING MYSTERIES!

SUZY!
RENA!
ELIJAH!
OH, THANK GOD!
THE ADULTS ARE HERE.

HELLO! WE'RE OVER HERE!

WHERE'S THAT BUILDING PLAN?

CAN'T YOU, LIKE, HOT-WIRE THE ELEVATOR?
WHAT? NO.

BUT YOU HOT-WIRED THAT SNOW TRUCK.
NO, I DIDN'T! I JUMPED A DEAD BATTERY!

IT'S A COMPLETELY DIFFERENT SITUATION.
HEY, I DON'T KNOW!

I WAS HIRED TO MAKE A MOVIE, REMEMBER?
UH, SUZY?

LEER

DID YOU KNOW YOUR OFFICE IS IN THE CENTER OF THE HOTEL?
SO?

SO . . .
HOW CAN IT POSSIBLY HAVE A WINDOW?

WE DETERMINED DANNY'S IN THE OLD HALCYON MINE.
WE JUST NEED TO FIND A WAY . . .

LEER
LEER
. . . DOWN THERE.

SUZY!
OOPS, BUSTED.
IT'S OK, MOM!
WE'RE FINE!
DRIP
ARE WE, THOUGH?
UGH! GROSS!
DRIP
I CAN'T SEE ANYTHING!
CAN YOU GET THE LIGHTS ON, RENA?
HOLD ON, I THINK I FOUND A FUSE BOX.
OUCH! MY FOOT!
THERE ARE LIGHTS?

I WOULDN'T BE MUCH OF A HOTEL MANAGER–
IF I COULDN'T BYPASS A BLOWN FUSE.

HOW FAR *COUGH* DOWN DID WE CLIMB?

FIVE . . . MAYBE SIX FLOORS.

HARD TO KNOW. WE'VE GONE OFF THE BUILDING PLANS.

LOOK AT THIS STEEL BOILER. GEESH.

THEY SURE DON'T MAKE 'EM LIKE THIS ANYMORE.

THIS MUST BE THE UNDERLOOKER'S BASE STATION.

LOOKS LIKE ONE OF YOUR MOM'S INVENTIONS.

IT SURE DOES.

I'M USING THE GALENA CRYSTAL YOU GAVE ELIJAH TO BOOST THE SIGNAL.
OF COURSE!
THE MOUNTAIN IS FILLED WITH GALENA. IT'S THE PERFECT CONDUCTOR.
MY DAUGHTER IS BRILLIANT!
YOU STILL THERE?
MOM?
SORRY! I'M HERE!
OK, YOU STAY RIGHT THERE; WE'RE WORKING ON THE ELEVATOR.
TRY THE BLUE TO THE RED.
YOWCH!
BZTN
DID YOU FIND DANNY?
NOT YET. WE HAVE TO GO DEEPER.
SUZY, LISTEN TO ME. THAT MINE AIR IS FILLED WITH CARBON DUST.
EVERY BREATH YOU TAKE IS SHORTENING YOUR LIFE.

YOUR MOM'S RIGHT. Y'ALL NEED MASKS.
THAT T-SHIRT IS COTTON, RIGHT?
YEAH.
NO!
NO
NO
IF THIS AIR WASN'T POISON, I'D BE SO MAD RIGHT NOW!
LOOK! FOOTPRINTS!
COME ON!

SURFACE
THIS WAY.
I AM THE GIRL IN THE CAVE.
COME ON, SUZY!

STAY OUT
STAY ALIVE
THROUGH HERE.

COUGH
DANNY!
WHOA! RENA!
HOW'D YOU GET DOWN HERE?!
WE'LL EXPLAIN LATER. RIGHT NOW WE NEED TO GO.
BUT I WANT YOU TO MEET MY FRIEND WARD!
HELLO, FRIENDS.

YOU BROUGHT THE FILMMAKER TO DOCUMENT OUR DISCOVERY!
I WOULDN'T WASTE A FRAME OF FILM ON YOU, CREEPAZOID!
HEY, DON'T CALL HIM THAT.
HE'S ON OUR TEAM!
WHAT IS THIS PLACE?
THIS IS ESTES PARK'S FORGOTTEN GOLD MINE.
NOW WE CAN REALLY SAVE THE HOTEL! HECK, WE CAN SAVE THE WHOLE TOWN.
WHAT'S WRONG, MISS HALLORANN? YOU DON'T SEEM VERY ENTHUSED.
OH, DID YOU NOT HEAR THE NEWS? THE GOLD RUSH IS OVER.
AS THE TRUE CARETAKER OF THE UNDERLOOK, SURELY YOU BELIEVE IT HAS MORE TO OFFER THAN A COLLECTION OF OLD FILMS.
ONLY THING I BELIEVE IN IS TEAMWORK . . .
. . . AND VAMPIRES ARE NOT TEAM PLAYERS.

DID YOU KNOW THAT SIX GOLD MINES WERE DISCOVERED WITHIN 100 MILES OF ESTES PARK? WHY CAN'T WE HAVE ONE?!
NO ONE'S SAYING IT'S NOT POSSIBLE.

BUT YOU'VE DONE YOUR PART, DANNY. GO BACK WITH RENA.
I WANT TO STAY AND HELP!
HALCYON

NO.
IT'S TIME TO MOVE ON.

WHAT ABOUT YOU?
I'LL BE RIGHT BEHIND YOU.

ELIJAH—
I'M NOT LEAVING WITHOUT HER.

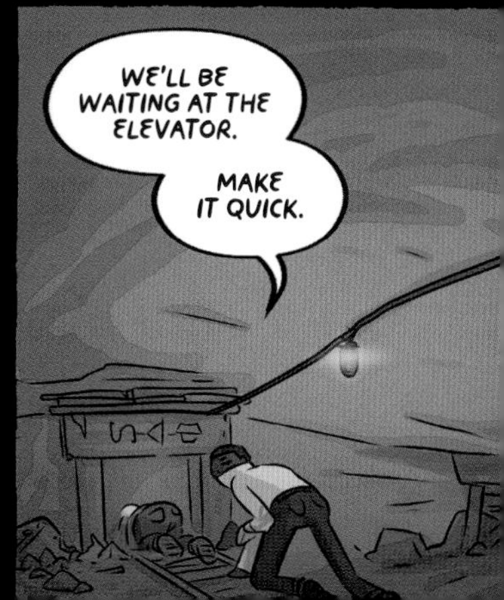
WE'LL BE WAITING AT THE ELEVATOR.
MAKE IT QUICK.

YOU LOOK LIKE YOU HAVE SOMETHING ON YOUR MIND, MS. HESS.
I WAS JUST THINKING HOW YOU'RE NOT THE FIRST TO TRY TO SAVE THE PARK.
LINDA LEER BELIEVED IN THE GOLD, TOO.

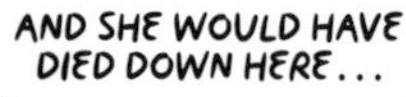
SHE CAME DOWN HERE FOR THE FIRST TIME WHEN SHE WAS A LITTLE KID.
AND SHE WOULD HAVE DIED DOWN HERE . . .
. . . IF SHE HADN'T HAD HER BEST FRIEND WITH HER.

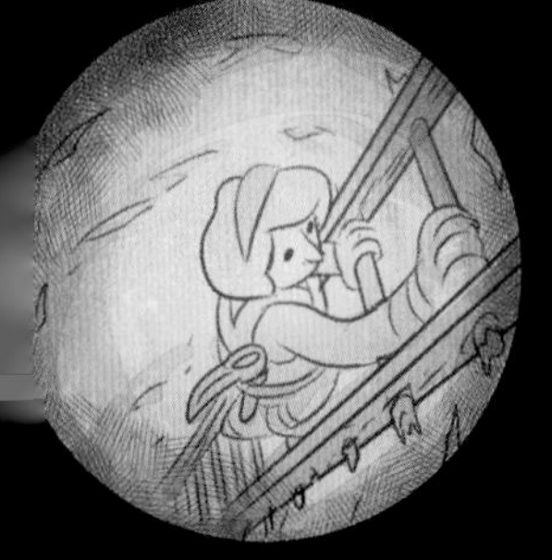

EDIE? WAS THAT YOU?

I HAD NO IDEA SHE KNEW THAT STORY.

THE ACCIDENT TRANSFORMED LINDA.
SHE BECAME AN INSPIRATION.
SHE BECAME FEARLESS IN EVERYTHING SHE SET HER MIND TO ACHIEVING.
A COMET!
AFTER THE FLOOD, SHE LED THE EFFORT TO REBUILD OUR PARK.
SHE WAS MY HERO.
AND SHE KNEW IT, TOO.
SHE SPENT HER FAMILY FORTUNE TRYING TO HELP US.
BUT IT WASN'T ENOUGH.
THAT'S WHEN THE GIRL RETURNED TO THE CAVE.

SHE BROUGHT ME DOWN HERE WHEN ALL SEEMED LOST.

SHE WANTED TO SHOW ME THAT HOPE COULD ALWAYS BE FOUND.

BUT I DIDN'T SEE HOPE. I SAW ONLY DEATH.

FOR YEARS I WAS ABLE TO BURY THE MEMORY OF THAT DARK DAY.
BUT NOW IT'S ALL I SEE.

I SEE THE FIGHT THAT CAME AFTER, MY MOM FURIOUS WITH LINDA.
I HEAR HER LAST WORDS TO HER BEST FRIEND—

"STAY AWAY FROM MY DAUGHTER."

AND SHE DID.
I NEVER SAW MY GODMOTHER AGAIN.

WHY ARE YOU TELLING ME THIS?
WELL, A WRITER SAID TO ME ONCE—STORIES BRING PEOPLE TOGETHER.
I NEVER TRUSTED WRITERS, BUT, YOU KNOW, MAYBE HE WAS RIGHT.
I MEAN, LOOK AT US. STRANGERS, TOGETHER, SLOWLY DYING IN A MAGICAL CAVE!
ENOUGH OF THIS! THEY NEED TO GET OUT OF THERE.
GIVE HER A MINUTE, EDIE.
BUT WHAT IS SHE DOING?!
TRYING TO SAVE A TROUBLED MAN.
FUNNY YOU SHOULD MENTION WRITERS.
BEFORE I BECAME A VAMPIRE, I CALLED MYSELF A WRITER.
ONLY MY STORIES NEVER DID ANYONE ANY GOOD.

IS THAT WHY YOU'RE HERE?
MAYBE. IT'S COMPLICATED.
HM.
"IT'S COMPLICATED."
THAT'S WHAT THEY SAID WHEN LINDA DIED.
BUT ACTUALLY, IT WAS QUITE SIMPLE.
SHE'D BEEN CURSED.
CURSED TO SEARCH THIS CAVE FOREVER–
LOOKING FOR A TREASURE WORTHY OF EVERYONE WHO HAD LOVED HER.
YOU WANT TO KNOW WHAT'S DOWN THERE, HUH?
VERY MUCH SO.

WELL, I'VE GOT THIS SPECIAL CAMERA.
IT CAN SHOW YOU UNSEEN THINGS.
IT'S BEAUTIFUL.
IT'S GALENA DUST.
THE STROBE LIGHT MAKES IT SPARKLE, BUT IT'S JUST DUST.
YOU KNOW THIS MOUNTAIN WILL TAKE EVERYTHING—
UNLESS YOU'RE HONEST ABOUT WHAT YOU'RE AFTER.
IF YOU'RE SO SMART, TELL ME... WHAT IS IT I'M AFTER?
SAME THING I AM...
...FORGIVENESS.

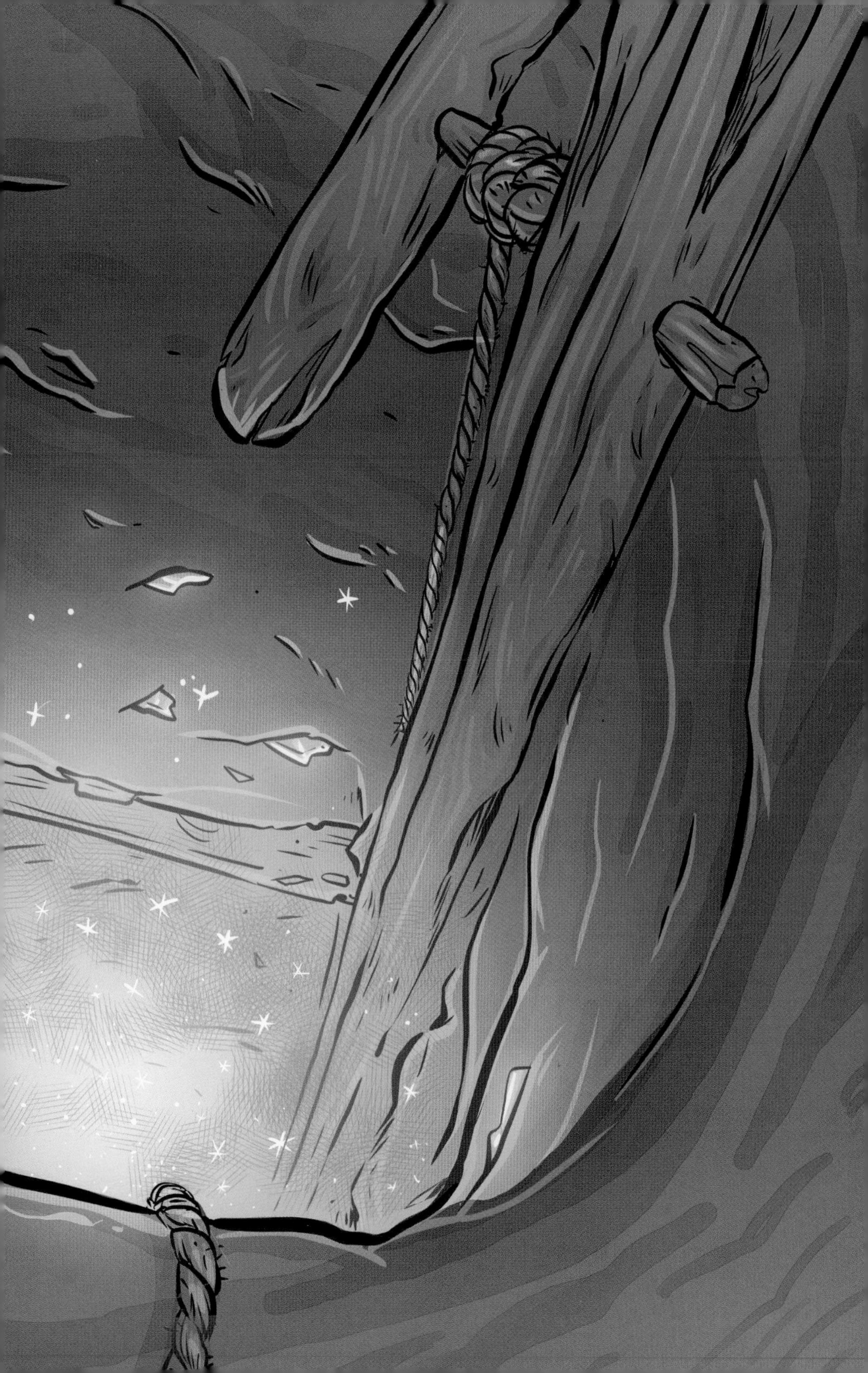

OK–
WE'RE COMING UP.
MR. AXWORTH!
GENE DOE, DENVER NEWS. I HAVE A FEW QUESTIONS . . .
DON'T YOU KNOW? HE DOESN'T DO INTERVIEWS!
WHERE'S YOUR INTEGRITY?!

THE CRIES OF DEAD MINERS!
WORSE!
IT'S FEEDBACK!
WHERE'S THE PLUG ON THIS DARN THING? IT'S GONNA OVERLOAD THE . . .
BZZT!
. . . FUSE BOX.
POP
POP
POP
POP

POP

UH-OH.

BZT

SURFACE
THIS WAY
SUZY?!
CAN YOU HEAR ME?

BZT!
WE'RE COMING TO GET YOU!

THUNK

HEY!
DON'T PLAY AROUND WITH THAT!

I'M NOT PLAYING!
I'M TRYING TO SAVE MY FRIENDS!

THE WATER'LL RUN DOWN THE TUNNEL.
THEY CAN FOLLOW IT OUT.

DANNY.

YOU'RE MY HERO.

NOW GIVE ME THAT–
AND STAND BACK.
COACH ALWAYS SAID I HAD A WILD SWING.
CRACK!

HM.
STILL GOT IT.
YEAH!

SPLOSH SPLOSH SPLOSH SPLOSH
COME ON!
SPLOSH

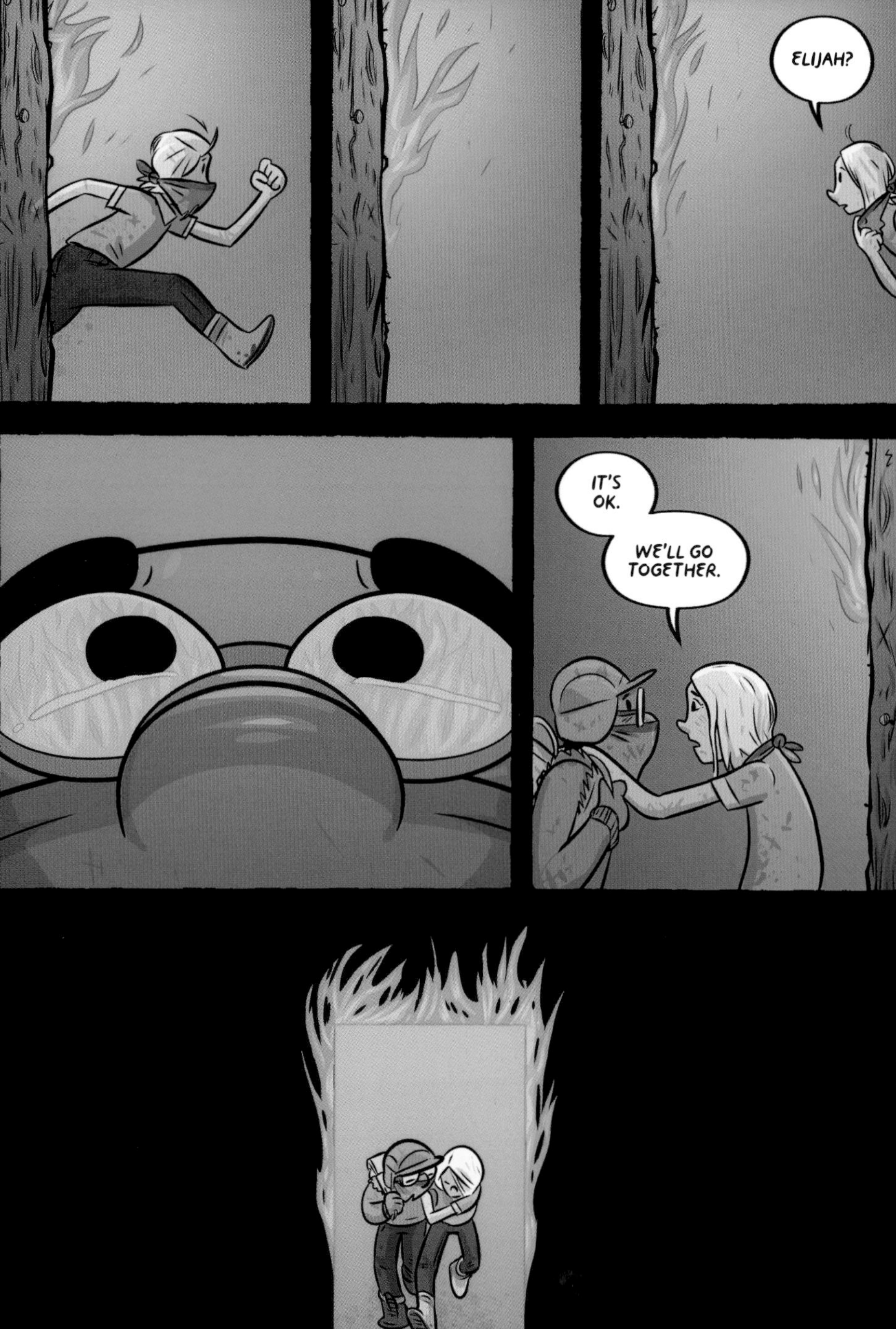
ELIJAH?
IT'S OK.
WE'LL GO TOGETHER.

WE GOTTA GO!
THIS PLACE IS A POWDER KEG!

IS THIS THING FAST ENOUGH?
WE'RE GOING TO BURN TO DEATH, AREN'T WE?!
NOT BEFORE WE CHOKE TO DEATH!

SUZY! WHAT ARE YOU DOING?!

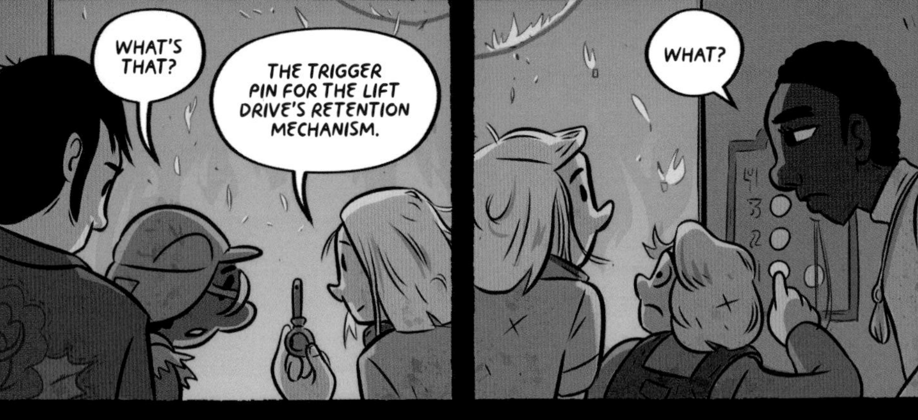
WHAT'S THAT?
THE TRIGGER PIN FOR THE LIFT DRIVE'S RETENTION MECHANISM.
WHAT?

I TURNED OFF THE BRAKES.

Ding

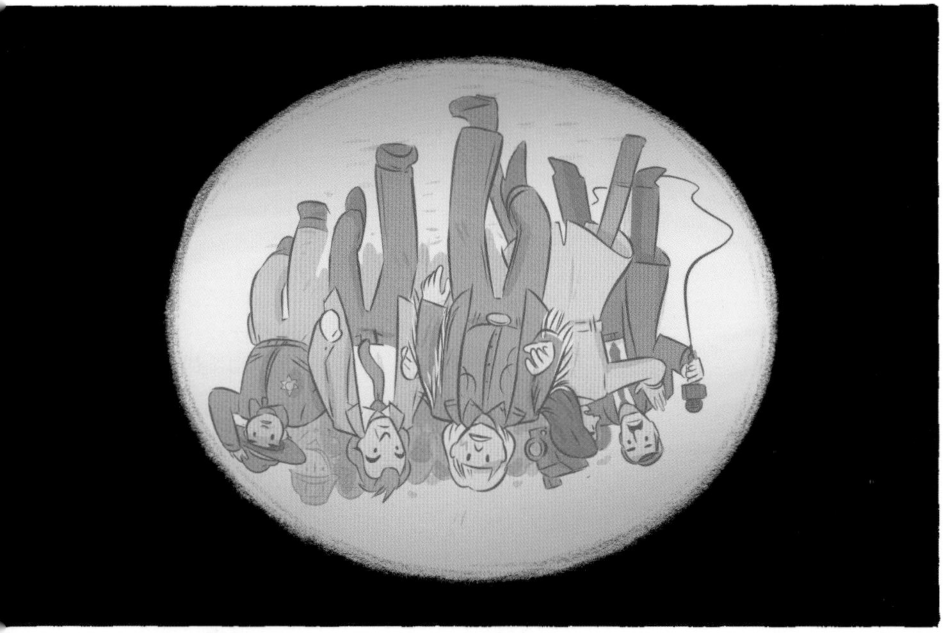

ESTES PARK, COLORADO

SATURDAY.

CREAKING COFFIN
JACK AXWORTH

AKLER

JACK AXWORTH
GARDEN OF THE GODS

The Underlooker
J. AXWORTH

JACK AXWORTH'S BEAST OF GLACIER CREEK

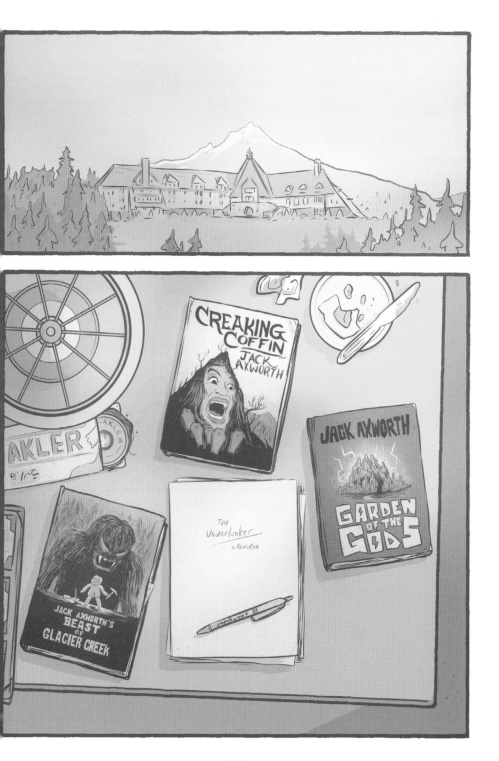

"All small towns have their secrets," he said. "You will no longer be one of them."

With those words, he pushed the stake through the vampire's heart. The monster fell dead. For the last time.

HA! WE'VE HEARD THAT ONE BEFORE.
ENDINGS ARE NOT EASY, YOU KNOW.
UGH! YOU'RE NO FUN!
RTY! PARTY! PART

BUT DAAAD!
YOU'RE NOT WEARING THAT TO THE PARTY!
NOW GO CHANGE!
HALLDRANN

UGH!
YOU'RE SO UNFAIR.

MMM, IT SMELLS LIKE HEAVEN IN HERE.
RED VELVET WITH CREAM-CHEESE FROSTING. YOU THINK SHE'LL LIKE IT?
SHE'LL THINK IT'S ABSOLUTELY WONDERFUL.

LINDA!

HEY, TODAY'S GOING TO BE A BIG DAY, SO I REALLY NEED YOUR HELP.
ANYTHING.

I'M SUPPOSED TO HELP YOU GET READY FOR THE PARTY.
NOW STOP WIGGLING.
I SAW A RABBIT RUN INTO THE MAZE!
WE HAVE TO HELP HIM!
NO, DANNY. YOUR MOM SAID–
BUT–BUT WHAT IF HE GETS LOST?
WE CAN'T LET THAT HAPPEN!
CAN WE?

HE'S NOT
REALLY A VAMPIRE,
YOU KNOW!

SUZY!
TELL THEM!
LET US HANDLE IT, KID.

HE'LL BE FINE.
HE'S JUST ANOTHER UNDERLURKER.

WOULD YOU TELL MR. AXWORTH, TELL EVERYONE—

I'M SORRY.

MIDNIGHT STAR
THE CURSE OF THE UNDERLOOKER
BY EDWARD BARLOW
RLOOKER
BY EDWARD BARLOW
YOU'RE KIDDING ME, SUZ!

WARD, THE VAMPIRE TOUR GUIDE...
...IS THE JOURNALIST EDWARD BARLOW?!
HE BLAMED HIMSELF FOR RUINING JACK'S CAREER.

I SHOULD HAVE FIGURED IT OUT BEFORE!
I COULD HAVE HELPED HIM!

SUZ, IT'S NOT UP TO YOU TO SAVE OUR TOWN.

IT'S OK TO JUST BE A KID SOMETIMES.

YOU REALIZE YOU'RE THE ONLY ONE WHO GOT THE WHOLE STORY?
YEAH.

AND YOU'RE JUST GOING TO LET IT GO? JUST LIKE THAT?
YEAH.

THAT'S INTEGRITY.

REMIND ME, RENA. HAVE I EVER SHOWN MY APPRECIATION FOR ALL YOU'VE DONE?
DON'T WORRY ABOUT IT, JACK. WE'RE ALL GOOD.

I WANT YOU TO HAVE THE HOTEL.
THAT'S NICE, JACK.
BUT YOU'VE ALREADY SIGNED IT OVER TO THE MUSEUM.

THE FILM ARCHIVE IS BURNING AS WE SPEAK.
I BELIEVE THAT CANCELS OUR CONTRACT.
WOW. YOU'RE SERIOUS.

I DON'T KNOW WHAT TO SAY.

SAY THAT YOU'LL TEAR IT DOWN AND BUILD SOMETHING OF YOUR OWN.
TEAR DOWN THE HOTEL. ARE YOU KIDDING?

IT JUST PLAYED ITS BEST GAME.

I CAN'T BELIEVE YOU'RE LEAVING TODAY.
IT FEELS LIKE YOU JUST GOT HERE.
I DUNNO, IT REALLY FEELS LIKE A WEE–
OOF!
YOU'LL WRITE ME, RIGHT?
YEAH. I CAN DO THAT.

I DON'T THINK JACK NEEDS TO REMEMBER THIS PART, ELIJAH.

THIS PART ISN'T FOR HIM.

THE BIGGEST THANK-YOU TO ANDREA COLVIN FOR WANDERING WITH ME THROUGH THE ~~MAZE~~ LABYRINTH THAT EVENTUALLY BECAME THIS BOOK.

THANK YOU TO MEGAN, JAKE, ADDISON, AND ARIA FOR ALL THEIR HARD WORK AND TALENT. SPECIAL THANKS TO ADRIANN FOR KEEPING AN EYE ON EVERYTHING.

AND A FOREVER THANK-YOU TO DOTTIE AND MAURA, WHO ARE ALWAYS UP FOR AN AFTERNOON WALK; GARVEY, WHO IS ALWAYS HUNGRY WHEN WE GET HOME; AND RESTY, WHO IS ALWAYS WITH US ♥

ABOUT THE AUTHOR

IRA MARCKS IS A CARTOONIST AND THE AUTHOR-ILLUSTRATOR OF *SHARK SUMMER* AND *SPIRIT WEEK*. HE LIVES IN UPSTATE NEW YORK WITH HIS WIFE, A CAT, A DOG, AND LOTS OF BOOKS HE'S BEEN MEANING TO READ.